THE SHEIKH'S
REBELLIOUS
MISTRESS

THE SHEIKH'S REBELLIOUS MISTRESS

BY

SANDRA MARTON

MILLS & BOON®

Pure reading pleasure™

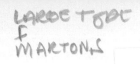
All the characters in this book have no existence outside the imagination of the author, and have no relation whatsoever to anyone bearing the same name or names. They are not even distantly inspired by any individual known or unknown to the author, and all the incidents are pure invention.

First published in Great Britain 2008
Large Print edition 2009
Harlequin Mills & Boon Limited,
Eton House, 18-24 Paradise Road,
Richmond, Surrey TW9 1SR

© Sandra Marton 2008

ISBN: 978 0 263 20596 1

Set in Times Roman 16½ on 19 pt.
16-0609-50501

Printed and bound in Great Britain
by CPI Antony Rowe, Chippenham, Wiltshire

CHAPTER ONE

IT WAS the sort of December afternoon that touched Fifth Avenue with magic.

Dusk had not yet fallen but the streetlights had already blinked on, gilding the fat snowdrops that fell lazily from the sky. Windows glowed with honeyed warmth from the multimillion dollar condos that filled the high-rise buildings lining the fabled street. Across the way, Central Park glittered under its soft dusting of white.

It was enough to make even jaded New Yorkers smile but not the man who stood at a window sixteen stories above the scene.

Why would a man smile when he was consumed by cold rage?

Sheikh Salim al Taj, crown prince of the Kingdom of Senahdar, Lion of the Alhandra Desert and Guardian of his Nation, stood motionless, a Baccarat snifter of brandy clutched in his hand. A casual observer might have thought his pale blue eyes were fixed on the scene below. The truth was, he'd hardly noticed it.

His vision was turned inward. He was reliving what had happened five long months ago until a sudden flash of movement brought him back to the present.

It was a hawk.

For a moment, the wild creature seemed poised in midair. Then it dropped gracefully on to the parapet of the terrace beyond the window, clinging to it with razor-sharp talons as it had done so often these past months.

The hawk didn't belong in the city. It certainly didn't belong in these concrete canyons at this time of year but the bird, like Salim, was a survivor.

Salim felt some of his tension ease. He smiled, lifted his glass in silent salute, then drank deep of the amber liquid it held.

He was not a sentimentalist. Sentimentality was a weakness. He was, however, a man who admired courage, resolve and single-minded determination. The hawk embodied all those qualities. It had survived in this alien setting; hell, it had flourished.

So had he.

Perhaps the metaphor was self-indulgent. Still, it was impossible to avoid. Salim was many things, not all of them good as these last months had proven, but he was not given to avoidance. Reality had to be faced, no matter what the consequences.

Outside, on the parapet, the hawk ruffled its brown and amber feathers and fixed its blazing eyes on the park. Night would descend soon; the hawk was readying itself for its final hunt of the day.

Would the hunt be successful? Salim had no doubt that it would. The creature was a predator. A consummate hunter whose cool intent, when properly focused, spelled doom for its fleeing prey.

Another metaphor, Salim thought, and felt a muscle tic high in his cheek.

The hawk had appeared a year ago, soaring effortlessly over the snarled traffic, then landing on the parapet as Salim watched.

The sight had startled him.

He knew hawks well. He had raised them, trained them, flown them in the mountains and deserts of Senahdar. He knew their courage. Their independence. The elegant savagery that beat in their blood, no matter how calmly they learned to sit on a man's fist.

Watching the bird, he'd felt a wrenching sorrow at what would surely be its fate. A wild creature could not survive here.

Wrong.

The hawk had claimed the elegant avenue and the park as its own, dominating them as it would have dominated the forests or deserts that surely should have been its home. Salim had gladly given over the terrace. There were two others—one on each floor of his triplex; he was more than willing to share ownership of one with his wild guest.

The hawk thrived on solitude and by trusting its own instincts. It would never let anything defeat it.

Salim's smile faded.

Neither would he. He'd been made a fool of five months before and the insult would be dealt with, and soon. Lifting the brandy snifter to his lips, he let the last of the liquid's fire sear his throat.

It still infuriated him to remember. How he had been lied to. How he had fallen for the oldest game in the world.

How the woman had humiliated him.

She had lied to him in the worst way possible. She had played a game in his arms, the kind he'd never believed he would fall victim to.

She had lied to him with her body.

Her sighs. Her moans. The little whispers that had driven him crazy.

Yes, oh, yes. Do that again. Touch me, there, Salim. Ah. Ah, like that. Like that. Just…yes. Your mouth. Your hands…

Damn it!

Just remembering turned him hard. Lies, all of it but still, he couldn't forget the feel of her. All that silken heat. The sweetness of her mouth. The weight of her breasts in his hands.

None of it had been real. Her sexual appetite, yes. But her hunger for him—for him, not for what or who he was—had been a lie. She had deceived him, toyed with him, made him blind to the truth.

Made it possible for her to steal his honor.

How else to describe waking up one morning to discover that she was gone and with her, ten million dollars?

A tremor of pure rage shot through him. He turned his back to the window, crossed the elegant room to a wall-length teak cabinet. The bottle of Courvoisier stood where he'd left it; he unstoppered it and poured himself a second drink.

All right. Part of that was an overstatement. He had not actually awakened to find Grace gone. How could he, when they'd never spent the entire night together?

Salim frowned.

Well, once. Twice, perhaps. Not more than that, and those times he'd stayed the night because of the weather or the lateness of the hour. Never for any other reason. She had her apartment. He had his. That was the way he liked it, always, no matter how long an affair lasted. Too much togetherness, no matter how good the sex, invariably led to familiarity and familiarity led to boredom.

That last time, he'd left her bed on a Friday night, flown to the West Coast on business. And when he'd returned to New York a week later, she was gone. So was the ten million, embezzled from the investment firm he'd built into a worldwide power.

Embezzled from an account inaccessible to anyone but him.

Salim took a long drink of the brandy, turned and walked slowly to the wall of glass. The snow had eased; the hawk was still perched on the parapet, motionless except for the slight ruffling of its brown, gray and amber feathers.

Ten million dollars, none of it found or recovered. The woman who'd stolen it had not been found, either. But she would be. Oh, yes, she would be, and very soon.

It was all he'd been able to think about today, after the call from the private detective he'd hired after the police and the FBI had proven useless. It was all he could think about now, as he waited for the man to arrive.

Five months. Twenty weeks. One hundred and forty-something days…and now, finally, he would get what he hungered for, an old concept his ancestors would surely have approved.

Vengeance.

Another swallow of brandy. It left a trail of smooth flame as it went down his throat but the truth was, nothing could warm him. Not anymore. Not until he finished what had begun last summer, when he'd taken Grace Hudson as his mistress.

Nothing unusual in that.

He was male, he was in his sexual prime, he was—why be foolishly modest?—he was a man who'd never had to go searching for women. They'd discovered him at sixteen, back home in Senahdar; if he'd been without a woman at any time since, it had been by choice, not necessity.

It was his selection of Grace as his mistress that had been unusual.

The women he took as lovers were invariably beautiful. He especially liked petite brunettes. They were also invariably charming. Why shouldn't a woman go out of her way to please a man? He was modern; he had been educated in the States but tradition was tradition and a woman who knew that it was important to cater to a man's wishes was a woman capable of holding a man's interest.

Grace had been none of those things.

She was tall. Five-eight, five-nine—still only up to his shoulder, even in the stiletto heels she favored, but there was no way one would describe her as "petite."

Her hair was not dark—it was tawny. The first time he'd seen her, his fingers had ached to take the pins from it and let it down and when, finally, he had, she had reminded him of a magnificent lioness.

As for going out of her way to please a man…She didn't go out of her way to please anyone. She was polite, well-spoken, but she was as direct as any man Salim had ever known. She had opinions on everything and never hesitated to state them.

She was a beautiful, enigmatic challenge. Not once had she sent out the signals women did when they were interested in a man.

Now, of course, he knew the reason. She'd been plotting from the start, cleverly baiting the trap. He hadn't seen it. He'd only seen that she was different.

Salim's jaw tightened.

Damned right, she was different.

She'd worked for him.

He never mixed business with pleasure. You didn't work and play in the same place. If you did, it was a surefire prescription for trouble. He'd always known that.

An unexpected event had brought her into his life. His chief financial officer—a staid, almost dour bachelor with a comb-over, thick glasses and no sense of humor—had stumbled into a midlife crisis that involved a bottle blonde and a Porsche. One day, the man was at his desk. The next, he was living with Blondie in a Miami condo.

Everyone had laughed.

"Lost his marbles over a babe," Salim had heard someone say. He'd chuckled right along with everyone else but the situation was serious. They needed a replacement, and quickly. Salim did what was logical, promoted the assistant CFO, Thomas Shipley, to the top job.

That left another hole in the organizational chart. Now his new CFO needed an assistant.

"Dominoes," the new CFO said with an apologetic shrug, but Salim knew it was the truth. He told him to hire someone. Such a simple thing. Such a damned simple thing…

Hell. The brandy snifter was empty again. Salim went to the bar and refilled it. Where was the detective? Their appointment was for four-thirty. He looked at his watch. It was barely four. His impatience was getting to him.

Calm down, he told himself. He had waited this long; he could wait just a little longer.

Outside, the long darkness of the winter night was setting in; it was time to switch on the lights, but darkness better suited his mood.

Every detail of what had happened after he'd told his new CFO to hire an assistant remained vivid, including the moment two weeks later when Shipley stepped into his office.

"Good news," he'd said. "I've found three candidates. Any of them would be an excellent choice."

Salim was in the midst of a deal that involved a billion dollar takeover. He had no time for anything else.

"Why tell me?" he'd said brusquely. "Select one."

Shipley had demurred. "I'm new," he'd said, "and this assistant will be new, too. I'd rather not take complete responsibility, sir. I think you should make the final decision."

Salim had grumbled, but he knew Shipley was right. Alhandra Investments was, to use American parlance, his baby. He had founded it; he ran it. He granted his people full authority but he always made it clear he was to be kept in the loop and the loop he was dangling now would require working closely with his new assistant CFO.

He met with the three candidates the next day. They all had excellent CVs but the résumé of one was outstanding.

There was only one drawback.

She was a woman.

A woman, as assistant CFO? He was not biased against women—of course, he wasn't—but, really, how capable could a woman be when it came to the intricacies of corporate finance?

Extremely capable, as it turned out.

Grace Hudson had degrees from Cornell and Stanford. She had worked for two of the best firms on Wall Street. She was articulate, knowledgeable, and if she was also the most beautiful woman he'd ever seen, what did that matter?

Her manner was polite but reserved. So was his. There was that thing about never mixing business with pleasure and, besides, she wasn't his type.

The fact that the huskiness of her voice haunted his dreams that night, that he found himself wondering what she'd look like with that mass of tawny curls loose about her heart-shaped face, that during the interview he'd had one incredible instant wondering what she had on beneath her black Armani suit…

Not important, any of it. He told himself that, and he hired her.

Three months later, he bedded her.

It had been a Friday evening. They'd been working late, he offered her a ride home. She lived in Soho; he mentioned he'd been invited to a gallery showing in her neighborhood on Sunday. Would she like to go with him? He had not meant to make the suggestion but once he did, he told himself it was too late to rescind it. When she hesitated, he made a joke about how awful these things usually were and how she could save him from dying of boredom if she said "yes."

She laughed, said well, okay, why not? They exchanged a polite good-night.

They were polite on Sunday, too, right up until the second he took her home. Then their eyes met and he knew he'd been kidding himself, that though he'd never touched her save for shaking her hand the day he'd hired her, he'd been dreaming of her, hungering for her for weeks.

Without warning, he'd caught her by the shoulders and gathered her into his arms.

"No," she said, and then his mouth captured hers.

Her mouth was hot and sweet, her kisses as wild as his. It was as if he had never kissed a woman until that moment. The taste of her had been like a drug; the way her pupils widened until her eyes were pools of deepest black had made him want to drown in their depths.

"Salim," she'd whispered as he framed her face with his hands, "Salim, we shouldn't…"

His hands had slipped under her jacket, his fingertips grazing her nipples, and she'd made a little sound he'd never forget and a minute later he'd had her against the wall, her demure skirt pushed up to her hips, her lace panties torn aside and he was inside her, deep inside her, swallowing her cries with his mouth, moving, moving, claiming her as he had longed to do from the first and to hell with the fact that they were still in the hall outside her apartment and anyone could have come along to see them, to hell with right or wrong, to hell with propriety.

To hell with everything except the passion that had consumed them both.

She'd come in his arms and when they'd finally

been able to breathe again, she'd stabbed her key into the lock and he'd carried her to her bedroom and made love to her again and again and again.

He'd made love to her for the next three months. Wherever he could. In his bed. In hers. In the back of his limo with the privacy partition drawn. In a little New England inn and once in his office—in his *office,* that was how she'd bewitched him because she *had* bewitched him, drawn him down and down into a sea of desire that blinded him to everything.

Three months into their affair, she'd disappeared.

So had the ten million dollars and whatever illusions he'd been fool enough to harbor.

The crystal glass shattered in Salim's hand. Amber liquid splattered over the hardwood floor; shards of glass rained down. A trickle of blood welled in his palm and he yanked a pristine white linen handkerchief from the breast pocket of his suit, wrapped it around his hand and staunched the crimson flow.

"Damn it," he snarled, his voice sharp in the silence of the penthouse.

At first, he'd turned his fury on Shipley. Hadn't the man vetted her CV properly? But Shipley had and Salim finally knew where his rage should be directed.

At himself.

He'd fallen for the oldest trick in the world. For a woman's wiles. Fallen for the lies, the scheming duplicity of a beautiful woman who knew how to use sex to blind a man to the truth…and why in hell was he going through the details again?

He knew them all too well, had gone over them more times than seemed possible, told them to the police, the FBI, the private investigator, endured the humiliation of seeing their sly looks when he had to say, yes, he had been involved with her, yes, they'd had an affair, yes, she'd had access to his home study, his desk, his papers, his computer…

No one could find her or the money.

Then, this morning, the P.I. had phoned.

"Your highness," he'd said, "we have located Miss Hudson."

Salim had taken a deep breath and arranged to meet the man. Here. At home. No one at the office talked about what had happened—none of his employees were fools—but he'd be damned if he'd discuss any of this at work.

Sudden movement caught his attention. The hawk sprang into the air; one beat of its powerful wings and it was above Fifth Avenue. Another, and it was silhouetted against the darkening sky over the park.

If the bird was going to make a successful takedown, it would have to do it now.

The intercom gave a polite buzz. Salim looked at his watch. The detective was early. That was fine. The sooner he had the information he needed, the better.

"Yes?" he said, lifting the intercom's handset.

"A Mr. John Taggart to see you, sir."

"Send him up."

Salim stepped into the marble entryway, folded his arms and waited. Moments later, the doors of the private elevator slid open and Taggart stepped out. He held a slim black leather portfolio under his arm.

"Your highness."

"Mr. Taggart."

The men shook hands; Salim motioned Taggart to precede him into the living room where Taggart looked at the spilled drink, the shards of glass, then at Salim's handkerchief-wrapped hand.

"An accident," Salim said. "Nothing to be concerned about. Do you want to take off your coat?"

Taggart answered by unzipping the portfolio, taking out a sheaf of papers and giving them to Salim. On top of the papers was a photograph.

Salim felt the floor give a quick tilt beneath his feet.

"Grace Hudson," Taggart said.

Salim nodded. As if he needed to be told. Of course it was Grace. She was standing on a street that might have been located in any city, wearing a suit and high heels and she looked guileless and innocent and, damn her to hell, she was neither.

"She's living in San Francisco under the name Grace Hunter."

Salim looked up. "She's in California?"

"Yes, sir. Lives there. Works for a private bank. She's their chief auditor."

A step down from the assistant CFO of Alhandra Investments but then, Grace would have been unable to produce a letter of reference. Salim frowned. Not that she needed any. Ten million dollars, and his former mistress was working as an auditor?

"Hunter was her mother's maiden name, and the job gives her a low profile. It's a common enough pattern among smart thieves. Give it a year or two, she'll head to Brazil or the Caribbean and start spending the money."

Salim nodded. Grace was smart, all right. But not smart enough.

"How come the authorities couldn't locate her?"

The P.I. shrugged. "They have a lot of urgent stuff on their plates."

Salim looked at the photo again. Somehow, he'd expected her to look different. She didn't. She was still tall, still slender, with eyes that were neither brown nor green but something in between. All that spectacular hair was, as always, pulled to the crown of her head and carefully knotted.

He could remember the feel of that hair. Silky. Soft. How it curled lightly around his fingers. How it tumbled down her back when he undid the pins, the way it kissed her shoulders and the sweet, rosy nipples of her uptilted breasts.

"Does she have a lover?"

His voice was rough; the question surprised him. He hadn't known he was going to ask it.

The answer didn't matter but he was curious. He knew her sexual appetite. She was not a woman who would go long between men.

"I didn't check for that." Taggart gave a small smile. "Her boss seems pretty interested, though."

A fist seemed to slam into Salim's belly. "Meaning what?"

The investigator shrugged. "Sees her home some nights. And he's taking her with him to a conference in Bali. They'll be there a week." Another little smile. "You know how it is, your highness. Good-looking woman, man notices—"

Yes. He knew. Damned right, he knew. And now he knew, too, why she was working at the bank in San Francisco.

"Can't say I blame him, if you want my op—"

"I don't pay you for your opinion, Taggart."

The investigator swallowed hard. "No, sir. I didn't mean—" He cleared his throat. "Everything you need is in that file. The lady's address, the place where she works, even the name of the hotel in Bali where she and her boss…where that conference is being held."

Salim nodded stiffly. Why blame the messenger for the message? That Taggart was perceptive enough to see the truth about Grace when he hadn't was no one's fault but his own.

He put his hand lightly on the detective's shoulder and walked him toward the elevator.

"You've been most helpful."

"Do you want me to alert the authorities, Sheikh Salim?"

"I'll deal with this from now on."

Taggart nodded. "If you're going after her yourself, I can find out what kind of extradition arrangements we have with Bali."

A perceptive man, indeed.

"Just send me your final bill—and thank you for all you've done."

Taggart stepped into the elevator. Salim waited until the doors slid shut. Then he walked slowly through the living room to the window.

But why would he go after Grace himself? He had contacts at the State Department. They could bring her back; he would confront her once they did.

A blur of motion.

It was the hawk, plunging through the sky, talons extended toward a gray shape on the sidewalk. Its prey fluttered in the hawk's grip as the bird soared upward. By the time the hawk landed on the parapet, the gray shape was still.

The hawk looked around with fierce intensity, then bent to its well-earned reward. It had done what it was bred to do.

Salim's jaw tightened. And so would he.

He took his cell phone from his pocket, hit a speed-dial button. His pilot answered on the first ring.

"Sir?"

"How quickly can you ready the plane for a flight to Bali?"

"Bali," the pilot said, as if Salim had asked about a flight to Vermont. "No problem, your highness. All I have to do is figure out the refueling stops and then file a flight plan."

"Do it," Salim commanded.

Then he snapped the phone shut, cast one last glance at the hawk and hurried from the room.

CHAPTER TWO

GRACE HUDSON prided herself on being well-traveled.

She had studied at universities that offered overseas academic programs and she'd participated in them. On scholarship, of course, because it had been tough enough working at places like Hamburger Heaven and The Sweater Stop to earn money to pay her regular tuition. But she was a good student—why be unnecessarily modest?—and so she'd spent six months studying in London and another six months studying in Paris by the time she was twenty-two.

Then she'd interviewed for a brokerage firm in New York, spent a couple of years there before moving on to another. Both companies had sent her abroad on business. London again, and Paris, and Brussels and Dublin and Moscow.

She was not new to foreign destinations.

But Bali? Bali, halfway around the globe? A place of beautiful beaches, brilliant seas, lush sunshine? When she'd first heard that was where she was going, she was amazed. She was new to her job. Was James Lipton the Fourth—her boss preferred using his full name—really going to give her such an incredible opportunity?

She'd looked at the brochure he'd dropped on her desk again.

Seventh Annual SOPAC-PBA Conference, it said. Inside was a heady list of speakers and workshops.

"Surely you know what SOPAC-PBA is, Miss Hunter," Lipton had said in his usual cool tones.

Miss Hunter. The name still took her by surprise. She'd taken her mother's maiden name after—after New York. The name was close enough to her real name to feel comfortable and she figured she'd be using it for a while.

Not that she was really worried about being found…

"Miss Hunter? Must I explain it to you?"

Grace had shaken her head. "No, Mr. Lipton. SOPAC-PBA is the acronym for the South Pacific Private Banking Association."

"You can learn a great deal by attending this conference, Miss Hunter. Do you think you're up to it?"

"Yes, sir. I am."

Lipton nodded. "I suppose you're wondering why I've decided to send you."

What could she say to that? Nothing, as it turned out. Lipton answered the question himself.

"I am pleased with your work, Miss Hunter, and I've reason to believe our CFO might be leaving us soon. There's the possibility you might be moving up. The conference is an excellent place to learn and network."

Moving up. To a position she'd lost because she'd found out, all too late, she'd never really had it, that everything Salim had done had been for himself, for his own selfish needs…

"Miss Hunter?"

Grace had blinked. "Yes, Mr. Lipton?"

"Have your secretary make the arrangements for us both."

"Both?"

"Of course. I'm attending as well. It's an important event."

Grace had her secretary arrange the details but Lipton had frowned over the results. Why a commercial flight when the company had an arrangement with a jet charter service? And the hotel rooms…Why had a regular room been reserved for him when he would need the amenities a suite would afford for private meetings and working dinners?

Grace apologized and said she would inform her secretary to make the necessary changes. Lipton said he would instruct his P.A. to handle matters herself.

Grace knew she'd lost points and promised herself she'd make up for it by making full use of the learning and networking opportunities in Bali. After all, a job she liked might be about to become one she knew she would love. And Bali… she'd always wanted to see it. Not alone. She'd wanted to see it with someone she cared for. With a lover. With…

She told herself she had to stop letting the past intrude on the present. She had a good job, there was the hint of a better one in the offing and she was lucky to get the chance to attend such a high-powered conference.

The sole drawback was that she'd have to spend the best part of a week with James Lipton the Fourth. He was occasionally brusque but she could handle that. There was something about him she just didn't like. Not his patrician air, not his attitude of removal. It was something else, something darker, something evil.

Which was ridiculous.

Lipton was a pillar of the community. There was an arts center named after him and a stadium. His wife was on the boards of half a dozen charities.

By the time she buckled her seat belt on the chartered jet, Grace had mentally called herself every kind of fool. She didn't have to like the man, she had only to respect his position as her employer.

That was it… At least, that was it until the plane was in the air.

It turned out that James Lipton the Fourth, that pillar of the community, wasn't a pillar at all. He belonged at the bottom of its most rancid garbage dump. To call him a sleazebag was being generous.

Twenty minutes after leaving San Francisco, the pilot announced they'd reached cruising altitude and her dipped-in-starch employer morphed into a monster.

They were seated side by side. He had suggested the arrangement. "So we can go over some notes," he'd said.

Logical enough.

What was not logical was the moment he leaned into her, his shoulder against hers, and said that if she grew weary during the flight, she could use the private bedroom in the rear of the plane.

"Thank you, sir, but—"

"With me in it, of course," he added.

Or had he?

At first, it seemed impossible. Grace decided she'd misunderstood him. Maybe the whine of the engines had distorted his words. So, she didn't reply.

But there was no way to misunderstand the fingers that drifted across her breast when he reached for a book, the hand that dropped on her

thigh when he asked about a report, the lascivi-
ous flick of his disgustingly wet tongue across
his disgustingly wet lips when she caught him
watching her.

Still, Grace tried to convince herself her imagination was playing tricks. That might easily
happen to a woman who had a decidedly jaun-
diced opinion of men.

She played it safe.

She retreated into work. Or pseudo-work. She
stared at her laptop's screen until she was afraid
her eyes would cross. When Lipton finally left
her side to use the toilet, she slammed down the
cover of her computer, scurried across the aisle
to a single leather seat, put her head back, closed
her eyes and pretended to sleep until the pilot announced they were ten minutes from landing,
which they did at four in the afternoon.

By four-fifteen, Grace knew she hadn't misunderstood anything. The pillar of the community had feet of clay. A bad metaphor but it
worked.

She had been duped.

Lipton had not brought her here to learn and
network. He'd brought her here so he could

seduce her, and that was as likely to happen as snow falling from the perfect Balinese sky.

A bright pink golf cart collected them at the airstrip. Lipton insisted on helping her into the cart; one of his hands brushed lightly over her buttocks as he did.

"Oops," he said, with his I-Am-A-Trustworthy-Banker smile.

Bull, she thought coldly...and then she thought, maybe it really had been an accident. Maybe her imagination was working overtime. How could Lipton be doing any of what she thought he was doing? The driver of the cart was right there, smiling politely. She had worked for Lipton all these months, spent late evenings poring over files and accounts with him and he'd behaved like a gentleman.

Was she letting the actions of the Don Juan of Senahdar color her thoughts? No. She hated Salim now; she always would, but until that Sunday evening they'd gone into each other's arms, he'd never done so much as touch her. No matter what else he was—unfeeling, arrogant, heartless—he would never have pawed a woman like this.

The golf cart deposited them at the hotel.

The first thing she saw when they entered the atrium lobby was a big sign that said Welcome SOPAC-PBA.

The second was a huge glass aviary filled with small, vividly colored birds.

And then she looked down and saw Lipton's arm as it snaked around her waist, his hand coming to rest just beneath her breast. She jerked away; his hand settled more firmly on her.

"Reception desk's right over there," he said briskly.

Grace looked at her boss. His eyes were on the desk, not her. It was as if he and the hand were not connected. What now? Struggle? Pull away? No time to do either. They reached the desk and Grace deftly sidestepped. Lipton's hand fell to his side.

The clerk flashed a toothy smile. Not at her. At her escort.

"Sir?"

"James Lipton the Fourth," Lipton said briskly.

"Of course. Mr. Lipton. Delighted to have you with us, sir. Welcome to Bali."

Still no acknowledgment of Grace, but why would there be? Lipton was the big attraction. She was invisible until he'd been dealt with. That was the way it went. Hadn't she seen it happen enough when she was with—with her prior employer?

Lipton didn't bother with niceties. "I take it my suite is ready?"

"Certainly, sir. If you'd be good enough to sign here… Excellent. Thank you." The clerk snapped his fingers. A boy dressed in a brightly flowered shirt and khaki shorts came running. "Wayan. Escort our guests to the Presidential Suite."

The boy reached for their luggage. Lipton reached for Grace. Grace did another quick sidestep.

"My name is Hud— My name is Hunter," she said pleasantly. "Grace Hunter. I have a reservation of my own."

"Nonsense," Lipton said, as if Grace weren't there. "Miss Hunter is my assistant. She will share my suite."

"I'm not your assistant," Grace said. "I'm the chief auditor of your bank."

What a stupid thing to say. The expression on the clerk's face said as much.

"I mean," she said carefully, "there's been an error. I arranged for—"

"Grace." Lipton spoke softly, but there was no mistaking the steel in his voice. "We are here on business. I have reserved a two bedroom, two bath suite. It has a dining room, a sitting room—all we'll require so we can confer whenever necessary and meet with other attendees in complete privacy. Do you have a problem with that?"

He made it sound so reasonable but yes, she had a problem…

"Grace?"

Lipton's eyes were as cold as his tone. What now? Make a scene in front of the bright-eyed desk clerk? Find a way to get back to San Francisco on her own? Lose the job it had taken her two months to land without a letter of reference?

No one knew better than she what it was like to be at the mercy of a ruthless, powerful man.

"Grace? I asked if you had a problem assisting me on this trip."

She looked at him. His expression was disdainful, his eyes icy. Grace took a deep breath.

"Not at all," she said politely. "Not when you explain it so well."

Lipton smiled. She was certain there were sharks with fewer teeth.

They followed the bellman to a suite that took up half the top floor. The boy pointed out the white sand beach, the view of the sea, the sixty-inch plasma TV, the Waterford chandeliers, the Gauguin prints on the walls.

The only things that mattered to Grace were that her bathroom was accessible only through her bedroom and that there was a lock on the bedroom door.

She secured it the second the boy left and, for two days, undid it only when she was ready to leave the suite. She ignored Lipton's suggestions she join him for drinks. For dinner. For break-fast. For anything and everything unless it involved other people. He made no comment, but the tension between them had grown palpable and she suspected he wasn't going to let things go on this way much longer.

But then, she wasn't going to give him a choice. He'd behave. He'd admit defeat.

That was possible, wasn't it? Maybe she was overreacting.

Grace gave an unladylike snort.

Powerful men, men who believed they owned the world, never admitted defeat. How could she have let herself be sucked into a situation like this? She'd been through this dance before.

The great career opportunity. The boss who seemed cold and reserved but began to unbend after a few after-hours meetings that certainly appeared to be strictly business, followed by a pleasant afternoon you couldn't even call a date. And then—and then—

A soft moan of despair rose in her throat.

"Liar," she whispered as she sank down on the edge of the bed. "Liar, liar, liar."

Grace took a deep, shuddering breath.

This wasn't the same at all.

She had never wanted Lipton's mouth on hers, his hands on her breasts, his body hard against hers. Never dreamed the kind of dreams she hadn't even known women had until she'd met one man, one gorgeous, exciting man. Until she'd gone to work for Salim al Taj and broken every rule she believed in by falling into his arms, his bed, by becoming his lover, becoming the kind of woman she knew he would never want.

Why think about that now? Months had gone

by. Their affair had ended just as it had started, with a suddenness that still shocked her. Not that she gave a damn. At least she'd salvaged her pride. He had tried to take it from her, but she'd put a stop to that, leaving him before he could leave her.

"Grace?" The rap at the door was sharp and imperious. So was Lipton's voice. "Grace. We have an appointment at eight." The doorknob rattled. "And I'm tired of this nonsense! There is no reason for this door to be locked."

There was every reason, just as there was every reason to quit this job as soon as they were back in the States. She'd find something else, even if it meant waiting on tables or clerking in a store. Both were honest ways to make a living and the people you dealt with weren't scum like her boss had turned out to be.

"Damn it, Grace, come out of that room at once!"

Grace smoothed the skirt of her pale green silk dress, picked up her purse, went to the door and opened it.

Her boss's expression was grim but his eyes, as they swept over her, glittered with heat. A tremor of fear went through her.

Something was going to happen tonight. She could feel it.

But it would not be what Lipton was planning. No matter what it took, it would not be that.

The appointment was legitimate enough.

Drinks with a few conference attendees in the hotel's lush gardens. Pleasant small talk, laughter, interspersed with discussions about the meetings they'd all attended during the day.

But Lipton made it more than that.

He stood as close to her as possible, his body brushing hers. His hand lay in the small of her back. His fingers drifted across hers when he handed her a drink she hadn't asked for and didn't want. He said "us" and "we" and used her name in a way that somehow lent it intimacy.

And, inevitably, people noticed. She saw the coolly assessing glances of the men, the way the women's eyes narrowed.

She sought a moment's solace in the ladies' room but when she was at the sink, washing her hands, one of the women in the little group came in and stood at the mirror beside her. Their eyes met in the glass.

"So," the woman said, with a little smile, "did you know he's married?"

"Did I know who is married?" Grace said, foolishly resorting to ignorance.

"Your, um, your *boss*," the woman purred, and gave a little laugh. "Perhaps you have hopes but, sweetie, trust me, it's not going anywhere. Stop playing coy and enjoy your stay here, if you know what I mean."

Grace turned off the water. The attendant pressed a soft linen towel into her hands.

"I know precisely what you mean," Grace said, willing herself to sound cool and calm when her heart was galloping. "And there's nothing about my stay here to enjoy, most especially not the company."

It was, she knew, a pathetic rejoinder but she wasn't one of those people who could turn clever when she was upset. She'd proven that in New York, running instead of facing her lover when she realized he was weary of her, that he was about to dump her from her job and his life with as little warning as you'd give a fly before you swatted it.

Her throat constricted.

"There you are." Lipton's hand closed around her arm. He smiled. His touch, his smile, spoke volumes. She could smell the whiskey on his breath. "Grace, you naughty girl, you forgot to remind me about the presentation I'm making in the morning."

"I *did* remind you," she said quietly. "Twice."

"Twice." Lipton grinned at the little group gathered around them. "She reminded me twice." His hand moved from her arm to her nape, his fingers curling around it. "Who would think a girl who looks like this would be concerned about her employer's calendar?"

Silence, embarrassed laughter and a couple of leering smiles greeted his slurred words. Grace spoke quietly.

"Let go of me."

"Now, darling, don't be silly. We're all friends here."

"Mr. Lipton. I said—"

"I heard you, darling. Now you hear me. I'm afraid we're going to have to pass on dinner with these charming people, go back to our suite and work on that speech." He chuckled. "Among other things."

Grace tried to move away from him. His hand clasped her nape more tightly.

One of the men cleared his throat. "I say, Lipton…"

"You say what?" Lipton challenged.

The man gave Grace a quick glance, then looked away. "Nothing," he said. "Nothing at all."

The people in the group began slipping away until, finally, Grace and her employer were alone.

"Let's go," he said, all his pretend charm gone.

"Damn you," Grace said, "get away from me. If you don't—"

"If I don't, what?" Lipton gave that shark's grin. "What will you do, Grace? Call for help? Make a fool of yourself in front of everyone? Lose not just your job with me but the chance of any job in finance?" Another grin. "Come on, darling, tell me exactly what it is you'll do if I don't get away from you."

"She won't have to do a thing," a male voice said. "I'll do it for her, Lipton, and when I'm finished, you'll be lucky if the doctors can put you back together again."

Lipton's hand dropped like a stone. Grace didn't move. Her heart was racing again. She knew that voice. Low. Masculine. Taut with command and, just now, icy with rage. God, yes. She knew that voice. Knew the man it belonged to.

She turned slowly and saw him. Tall. Dark-haired. Broad-shouldered. Eyes the palest shade of blue she had ever seen, nose straight as a blade, mouth firm, jaw clenched…

She knew him, all right.

This was the man who had broken her heart.

This was the crown prince of Senahdar.

This was the man she hated.

CHAPTER THREE

GRACE was looking at him as if he were an apparition.

Salim could hardly blame her.

She'd stolen a fortune, fled, taken a new name to cover her tracks. The last thing she'd expect would be a ghost from her past turning up in Bali. Her shock was a glorious thing to see, even though he'd intended their meeting to be more private.

He'd wanted to come upon her when she was alone. Vulnerable. At night, in her room. He'd planned to bribe a maid to let him enter it while Grace was at dinner.

He'd amused himself during the long flight, imagining how the scene would play.

Darkness outside the windows. Darkness in her room. He, waiting motionless. The snick of her key card in the lock, the door swinging open, then closing behind her. Before she could touch the light switch, he'd speak her name.

"Grace."

She would cry out and he would turn on a lamp so he could see the shock in her eyes. And then he would…

What?

What would he do, when they were alone in her room, she terrified, he triumphant? He'd spent hours thinking about it.

Imagined himself going toward her, telling her that he was taking her back to the States to face charges of embezzlement.

Imagined her panic at that news…and her reaction when he said that first, she was going to pay a very private penance.

He would tell her she had to strip for him, take off the businesslike suit or dress, the surprisingly delicate bits of silk she always wore beneath. Take those off, too, until she was naked. Until he could see the roundness of her breasts, the soft pink blush of her nipples, her flat belly and the delicate dark gold curls between her thighs.

"Now undress me," he'd say, and she would,

undoing his tie, his shirt, his trousers, her hands moving over him with the delicacy of butterfly wings. And when they were both naked, he would make her do all those things with her hands and mouth and body she had once claimed she did out of desire when the truth was, her desire had been not for his kisses, his arms, his possession but for ten million dollars of his money.

"Who do you think you are?"

Lipton's voice was sharp with aristocratic demand. For a minute, Salim had forgotten him. He knew the man by reputation. James Lipton the third or fourth or some such inane thing, a principled banker, an unprincipled seducer of young women. Interesting, that Lipton and Grace should have found each other.

Who would seduce whom?

"I asked you a question," Lipton said with presumptive authority. "Who are you? And how dare you intrude on a private conversation?"

"No," Grace said in a tremulous voice. She put her hand on Lipton's arm. "Mr. Lipton…"

"Mr. Lipton." Salim's lip curled. "Is that how you're playing it? Are you the terrified innocent this time, Grace? Did I interrupt the big seduction scene as opposed to saving you from the unwanted attention of a predator?"

"What did you call me?" Lipton sputtered.

"Salim. Please…"

Grace's boss swung toward her. "You know this man?"

"So many questions," Salim said coldly, his eyes locked on his adversary's. "Suppose we take them one at a time. What am I doing here? That's easy. I am here on business. Does your charming companion know me?" An icy smile. "She knows me very well. Intimately, one might say."

Grace felt her face heat.

"As for what I called you… I said you were a predator, Lipton, which might prove quite interesting, considering that the lady you've targeted bears the same distinction." He smiled tightly. "Which makes me wonder if her reaction to your pathetic attempts at seduction were real, or was she acting?"

It was an insult, but Grace knew it was also a question. All she had to do was tell Salim he had misinterpreted what he'd seen. She'd get rid of him, all right—and then she'd be trapped, alone, with her boss.

"As for who I am…" Another tight smile lifted the corners of Salim's lips. "My name is Salim al Taj."

No title. No "sheikh" or "prince." It wasn't necessary and her former lover knew it. Grace watched the color drain from Lipton's haughty face. A moment ago, he'd been puffed up with self-importance. Now, he looked terrified.

There was a time knowing her lover had such power would have thrilled her most basic female instincts. Now, it made her shudder.

"You mean—you mean you're the head of Alhandra Investments? You're the sheikh? The crown prince of Senahdar?"

"I see you've heard of me," Salim said with icy sarcasm.

Lipton swallowed hard. "Your majesty. Your highness. Sir. I—I beg your pardon. I had no idea the lady and you were—that the lady was— If I had known…"

"We are not," Grace said desperately, looking from one man to the other. "I mean, I am not— the sheikh and I are not—" What was that old saying? she thought frantically. Caught between the devil and the deep blue sea.

"Grace?"

She looked up at Salim. His pale blue eyes were cold; his smile made her feel cold but what choice did she really have?

"Salim and I," she told Lipton. "Salim and I are—are—"

Salim's arm curved around her waist.

"A lover's quarrel," he said dismissively. His sharp gaze met Grace's. "Isn't that right, *habiba,* or did I get it wrong? Perhaps you prefer to see me walk away."

Once, she'd have melted at the soft term of endearment. Now his tone gave it a twist that all but turned it into an obscenity.

"Crunch time, sweetheart," Salim said softly. "Make a decision and do it quickly."

A decision, she thought, and bit back a hysterical laugh. Send Salim away and be trapped with Lipton? She had no illusions about what he wanted.

She had no illusions about what Salim wanted, either.

Revenge.

A man like him wouldn't deal well with a dented ego. He was furious that she had left him without a word of explanation and, even worse, that she'd left him before he could leave her.

His arm tightened around her. "Well? Are you coming with me or shall I leave you here?"

He sounded like a man who knew a woman would never reject him, his question asked with almost lazy ease, but the pressure of his hand warned his patience was wearing thin. Logic told her she could only come to one decision. If she let Lipton see her go off with Salim, she wouldn't have to fear what he might try to do later, when they were alone again.

Grace took a deep breath. "Buy me a drink," she said brightly, as if Salim's description of things between them were true, "and we'll talk about old times."

Salim's eyes glittered. Old times, indeed.

He led her away from the lights of the hotel to a shell-strewn path that led to the beach. He had not expected her to make a decision that quickly. Perhaps the scene he'd stumbled across had actually been what it seemed: a pig of a man hitting on a woman who wanted no part of him. That had certainly been his initial reaction; it was why he'd stopped Lipton, why he wished to hell the man had come at him. He'd have taught him that a man should not treat a woman that way, any woman, even a liar and a cheat like Grace.

His desire to pound a fist into Lipton's gut had come from something far less sophisticated.

Mine, he had thought when he had seen Grace with another man's hands on her. He had reacted as any man would, seeing a woman he'd once called his with someone else touching her. That shot of masculine testosterone was not something one could control. It was built into male DNA; it wasn't about Grace in particular or who could or could not have her.

He didn't gave a damn who she seduced or who she slept with. All he cared about was getting her off this island and back to the States.

The sole question was how best to do it. He was prepared to use force, if he had to, but only as a last resort. He knew nothing of extradition arrangements between Bali and the U.S.A.; it had probably been foolish not to let Taggart check but he'd been blind to everything but getting here, finding this woman…

"Salim."

Finding her and making her pay for what she had done.

"Salim!"

Did she think she could stop him? That he'd lead her away from Lipton and release her? There wasn't a way in hell he'd do that. She was a thief. As for the rest, the fact that she'd left him…Yes, that bothered him. Why wouldn't it? Women came and went in a man's life but the time of leaving was up to the man. That was just how it was. How Nature intended it. Ending an affair was a man's prerogative, but that was not what this was all about.

"Are you deaf?" Grace demanded, trying to twist free of his encircling arm. "Let go of me!"

"Stop complaining," he growled, "and be grateful I didn't tell your would-be lover the truth about you."

"He's not my would-be lover, and what you know of truth could fit into a thimble!"

He spun her toward him so suddenly that she teetered on her spiked heels. His hands bit into her shoulders. To steady her? To let out some of his rage? It didn't matter. What mattered was the way the moonlight cast an ivory glow over her skin, the way her eyes glittered, her lips trembled.

He'd expected to find her… What? Looking like the criminal she was? Pale? Desperate? Driven? Instead she looked no different than when she had been his. Beautiful. Elegant. Innocent, and wasn't that a fine choice of words to use for such a woman?

What she had done to him had truly meant nothing to her. If anything, she was lovelier than ever, or was it only that his dreams of her were no match for the reality?

"Why are you looking at me like that?"

He barked a laugh. "Like what, *habiba?* How, exactly, is one supposed to look at a fugitive?"

Oh, the expression on her face was priceless! Stunned. Horrified. And then—and then, by Ishtar, was that a smile? Was she laughing? At him? Did she dare laugh at him?

Salim's grip on her tightened as he lifted her to her toes. "What are you laughing at?"

"You're hurting me!"

"Answer the question. What do you find so amusing?"

"You," Grace snapped. "You and that—that supersized ego."

"You want to discuss egos, *habiba?* How about yours? Did you really think you'd cover your trail so well that I wouldn't find you?"

"I didn't cover anything!"

"Really? Since when is your name Grace Hunter?"

"Since I figured out that I didn't want you finding me. Not that I really thought you'd even try. I mean, why would you give a damn that I'd decided our relationship had run its course?" She tossed her head, a gesture of defiance he remembered all too well. "You just didn't like me being the one who made the first move."

He hadn't liked it, not one bit. But that wasn't why he'd looked for her. He'd had ten million reasons to find her, and what she'd called a relationship was definitely not one of them.

"Leaving something out, aren't you, darling?" he said, his tone silken.

"Not a thing." She raised her chin. "Our affair ended. I knew it and so did you. What did I leave out?"

Salim's mouth thinned. He should have expected she'd react like this. Grace was not stupid. There was no way she would admit to the embezzlement and he wasn't a fool. This was not a bad TV movie; she would not blurt out the truth if he insisted on it.

"You left out the part where I find you and take you back to New York."

Her eyes widened. "Is that why you came here?"

"Did you think I came to be bored out of my mind at a conference?"

"But—but why would you want to take me to New York?"

"That's fine, Grace. Keep playing games." Salim tugged her toward him. She struggled but he was too tall, too big, too powerful. Her struggles got her nowhere except exactly where he'd wanted her, pressed tightly against him. "But they won't work. How many times do you think you can make a fool of the same man?"

"What are you talking about? Why would you think I'd agree to go back with you?"

"Who said anything about agreement?" His voice was low and dangerous. "You will go with me and face the consequences of your actions because it is what I demand, *habiba*."

She stared at him as if he'd lost his mind.

Maybe he had.

Holding her like this, so close against him, brought back far too many memories.

The feel of her in his arms. The softness of her breasts against his chest. The delicate flare of her hips. Even the remembered floral scent that was woman and Grace, a scent that brought back images of her moving beneath him, her skin heated by passion as he cupped her breasts, drew the pale pink nipples into his mouth…

"Don't," she whispered, and he realized he'd turned hard as stone, that his erection was pressed against her belly…

That she was looking up at him in a way that told him all he needed to know.

"Don't," she said again, and he cupped her face in one hand.

"Don't what, *habiba?*" he said thickly, and he stopped thinking, bent his head and sought her mouth.

In a second, in a heartbeat, she was his again.

Her lips parted under his. Her breath whispered against his mouth. Her hands rose, caught his dinner jacket, curled into the lapels as she rose to him.

Salim groaned. Grasped her skirt. Shoved it high on her thighs. Grace whispered something, pressed herself closer, whimpered as he slid his hand up her legs, between her thighs, cupped her, felt the sweet moisture of her arousal.

She was his. His, his, his…

What in hell was he doing?

Salim cursed, caught Grace by the shoulders and thrust her from him. She swayed unsteadily. Her dark lashes lifted. Her eyes had the blurred look of a woman swept away by desire, but he knew better. He had been the one in the raw clutches of desire; she had been the one who'd planned the scene.

"Damn you," he said in a hoarse whisper. "Do you really think that's going to work again?"

She stared at him, shook her head as if to clear it. Oh, she was good!

"What did you say?"

"You heard me. It won't work, *habiba*. I'm on to the game."

Her mouth trembled. She looked devastated. He fought back the stupid desire to take her in his arms again. Just as well. A second later, she was all cool composure. The vulnerable waif had been replaced by the real woman. He had to give her points for quick recovery.

"And so am I, Sheikh Salim. You've come all this distance for nothing. I am not going back to New York."

He smiled. "Really."

"I am not going to New York, and I have no intention of prolonging this discussion."

She turned on her heel and strode away. He waited, then called her name.

"Grace."

She didn't pause. Salim raised his voice.

"You have no choice, *habiba*. You're finished here."

That did the trick. She stopped walking and swung toward him.

"Ah," he said softly, "just look at your face, darling. Such an expression of shock. Really, though, what would you expect? Did you play Lipton along? Did you promise more than you intended to deliver? Is that what that little scene was all about?"

"How dare you say such a thing to me?"

"Maybe not. Maybe he really was hitting on you." Salim walked to where she stood, put his hand under her chin and jerked her head up. "But why should I care? The point is, I won't have to lift a finger to get you onto my plane and off this island now. You're in trouble, Grace. He's going to get even, either by using his influence against you…" His face lowered to hers. "Or by waiting for you at the hotel. He'll be all over you the minute he gets you alone."

Grace went very still. "No. He won't do anything. He's afraid of you."

"I humiliated him. There's a difference. He'll want to get even and if you walk away from me and go back to him, he'll figure I'm done with you. That will put him back in the game."

"You're despicable," she whispered, her voice trembling.

"I'm honest, *habiba*. I know how men are. Use your head," Salim said, his tone sharpening. "Do you really think he's going to pretend this didn't happen? His behavior with you, your reaction, my interference. He can't take it out on me, but he won't have to. He'll have you."

Tears shone in her eyes; one traced a path down her cheek. Salim fought the desire to gather her to him and comfort her. Only a fool would do that. Grace was an actress. A siren. Who knew that better than he?

"He won't have me," she said quickly. "I'm going back to the hotel, not to him."

"It's the same thing. You're sharing his room."

"His suite," she said, even more quickly. "A company suite. I didn't know anything about it until…" Grace clamped her lips together. Why was she explaining anything to Salim? Why was she letting him see her fear? See it? He was building on it. He didn't give a damn about her. He only wanted her acquiescence but then, there was nothing new in that. He was a man who always wanted things done his way.

And, right now, he was doing whatever it took to make that happen. Her boss was a vile human being but Salim was trying to convince her the man was a monster. Well, it wasn't going to work, she thought, and took a steadying breath.

"Let go of me," she said coolly.

He hesitated. Then, slowly, his hand fell to his side.

"Nicely done," she said with a little smile. "You almost had me in a panic. Sorry, but it won't work. Lipton's a pig, but there's not a woman alive who can't handle a pig on her own."

"You're always so sure of yourself, *habiba*. This time, though, you may be making a mistake. Just in case you are…" Salim took his key card from his pocket and tossed it to her. Grace caught it out of reflex. "I have one of the villas on the beach. Number 916."

"I wouldn't come to you if hell froze over."

Such a pathetic rejoinder, but it was the best she could manage. Head high, she turned and made her way up the path toward the gardens. Was Salim watching her? She wanted to look over her shoulder to find out, but she wouldn't give him the satisfaction.

What a cold-hearted bastard!

She'd always known that about him; she'd just refused to admit it. She'd told herself his arrogance was actually self-confidence. It wasn't. Only an arrogant man with an overblown ego would come around the world just to prove that a woman couldn't leave him until he was good and ready for it to happen.

That he actually believed she would fly to New York with him, that he saw her as a fugitive for leaving him…

Laughable, all of it.

Grace's steps slowed as she entered the garden.

If it was laughable, why had she let him kiss her? Why had she kissed him back? Why had her foolish heart wished, even for a moment, that he had come for her because he needed her?

Stupid to even think such a thing. Salim didn't need anyone. What he understood was passion. How to touch a woman so the most intimate part of her wept for his possession. How to make her beg for release.

And he knew how to respond. She didn't want to remember, but she did.

His hard-muscled body, taut and powerful against hers. His shudder of delight when she caressed him, his soft groan when she used her tongue, her lips to pleasure him. The incredible moment when he'd part her thighs, sink deep, deep inside her.

And yet, there were times she'd had the feeling he was there physically but not emotionally, that he'd kept a part of himself locked away…

"There you are."

She jumped as Lipton stepped out of the shadows. He caught her wrist, his fingers digging deep into the soft inner flesh.

"What happened, Grace? Didn't the reconciliation go well?"

Grace's heart was racing. It was difficult to pretend she wasn't frightened but she knew it was what she had to do.

"Let go of me," she said quietly.

"Or is it that the mighty sheikh only wanted a quickie on the beach? You'll find I'm not like that. I believe in hours of pleasure, Grace. Some women find it excessive, but I'm sure you won't be one of them."

"Get this through your head," she hissed. "I am not going to sleep with you."

"I hope not. Sleeping isn't what I have in mind."

Grace used the only ace in the deck. She didn't want to; falling back on Salim's name made her feel helpless but she couldn't see another way out.

"The sheikh will kill you if you touch me."

Lipton smiled. "He's finished with you, Grace. I don't see a problem."

His fingers moved to her upper arm; she felt their bite and she stifled a moan. What he was doing was incredibly painful, but she knew she'd sooner pass out from it than ask for mercy.

"You see, Grace, if he was a real threat to you and me—to our relationship…"

"We don't have a relationship!"

"Of course we do, and wait until you see how exciting it's going to be." Lipton leaned toward her; his breath, whiskey-laden before, was soaked with it now. "As I was saying, if your ex was a real threat, he'd have kept you for the night instead of taking you outside and then sending you packing."

"Let go of me or—"

"He did," Lipton said with glee. "Send you packing. Poor Grace. Things just didn't work out for you."

"Listen to me," Grace said. "If you think I'm afraid to make a scene—"

"That's exactly what I think, and I'm right. You don't want everyone to know what you've done, Grace. How you led me on. How you said you wanted to sleep with me." His fingers dug deeper into the tender muscle of her biceps; the pain sent nausea roiling in her belly. "Because if I told people that, the only job you'd be able to get in finance would be one that involved standing behind a cash register and saying 'Do you want fries with that?'"

Grace blinked. Then she laughed. She couldn't help it. Hadn't Hollywood once made movies like this? Cruel villains, helpless heroines…

Her laugh became a soft cry of pain as Lipton's fingers clamped harder on her arm.

"I'm going to have another drink with my friends while you go to my bedroom and make yourself ready for me. I'll be half an hour, not more, and when I open the door, you'd damned well better make this trip I paid for as well as tonight's humiliation worth my while."

"No. No! You'll never touch me. You'll never—"

Lipton backhanded her. Grace staggered. He came at her again and she summoned up the long-ago advice of her high school judo instructor.

A woman's knee makes an excellent weapon.

She moved quickly. Lipton grunted, gagged and fell back.

And Grace turned and ran.

CHAPTER FOUR

SALIM had been told that the hotel's villas were spacious and handsome.

Maybe, but he'd dismissed those amenities without a second thought. A man on his way to apprehend a thief didn't give a damn about aesthetics.

Now, as he paced the floor of his villa, he thought that "spacious" might be a good thing. You could only march from room to room just so long before the walls began closing in.

Where was Grace?

Salim glowered at his watch. Was it working? Of course it was. The gold Cartier had been passed from his grandfather to his father to him. It was entirely—and, tonight, unfortunately—dependable.

His common sense was not.

Why had he let Grace go back to the hotel and to Lipton? At the time, it had seemed eminently sensible. Let her get hold of her anger, he'd told himself. Let her stalk away, sulk, roar at the moon if she wanted. Once she came to her senses, she'd figure out she had no choice but to return to New York as his prisoner.

She was a thief, not a fool.

She knew she was caught. Her days of freedom were over. Why go through the hassle of extradition, assuming there was an extradition agreement between Indonesia and the States? Even if there wasn't, what she'd done would become public knowledge. The media would be all over the story. She had to see there was no sense fighting the inevitable.

As for putting herself in Lipton's hands… No. She wouldn't do that. Salim had pretty much decided she'd told the truth, that she hadn't been leading the banker on.

It was logical, then, to have given her enough space to come to her senses.

Completely logical…except, if it was, then where was she?

"Stop it," Salim said, his voice a raspy growl in the silence of the villa.

He was working himself into a state over nothing. So what if this wasn't playing as he'd figured? It didn't matter if Grace came to him or if he went and collected her in the morning. She wasn't going anywhere. There was no way off this bit of Bali except by private plane or boat, and he'd used a significant number of Euros to ensure that men at both the small airport and marina were watching for her and would phone him if she appeared.

Right. Then, why was he damned near leaving footprints in the marble floors of the villa?

Because everything would be simpler if she came to him.

He'd call his pilot, tell him to ready the plane. There'd be no need to get Grace out of the hotel without a scene, no reason to hustle her to the plane by using his title to convince people to look the other way when he did it. No question, if she came to him willingly, there'd be fewer complications.

Salim stopped pacing. A muscle knotted in his jaw.

"How about the truth?" he muttered.

Yes. How about the truth? How about acknowledging, at least to himself, that if Grace did this the way he wanted, it would humble her. Not that he could imagine Grace really humbled. She was too proud for that. It would humiliate her. It would be a symbol of her defeat, and what was wrong with that?

Being humiliated was only the start of what she owed him. Maybe it was petty but...

Salim scowled, dug his hands into his trouser pockets and resumed his endless walk to nowhere.

It wasn't petty. It was logical. Hadn't he already come to that conclusion? Unless she left with him willingly, he'd have a scene on his hands. She'd protest, yell, maybe even kick and scream...

And he'd know just the way to subdue her.

He'd drag her into his arms and cover her mouth with his.

She'd struggle, maybe even try to bite him but, in the end, she'd stop fighting and melt into his kiss the way she'd done a little while ago.

God, that kiss.

Her soft mouth. Her sighs. Her moans. So

familiar and yet always more than enough to turn him on.

Or had she been faking her response? Had she faked it when she was his mistress? He wasn't a fool; he knew a woman could fake pleasure, but could Grace fake the way her nipples beaded at the brush of his fingers? Could she fake the moist heat that had always greeted him when he put his hand, his mouth, between her thighs?

What in hell was he doing? Thinking himself into arousal at a moment like this was just plain stupid, especially over a woman he didn't want…and he was tired of trying to figure out what was going on. Why drive himself crazy when there was an easy way to find out?

Salim grabbed the house phone and hit the button for the concierge.

"This is Sheikh al Taj," he said brusquely. "I'm looking for one of your guests. Grace Hud— Grace Hunter. Have you seen her?"

"No, sir, I haven't."

"What about James Lipton? Have you seen him?"

"As far as I know, sir, Mr. Lipton is in the garden."

Lipton was in the garden. Grace would have to

pass through it to reach the hotel but she hadn't shown up yet. Surely she'd had plenty of time to make that relatively short walk…

"Your highness? Would you like me to page Miss Hunter? Or Mr. Lipton?"

"That won't be necessary," Salim said, and slammed down the phone.

There was nothing mysterious in the fact that Grace wasn't at the hotel. The hotel grounds had several lit paths; she was angry and maybe she'd decided to walk for a while to calm down. Or maybe she'd decided to take her chances with her boss instead of him. Fine. It changed nothing. She would still go back with him tomorrow; nothing she could do would change that.

It wasn't his problem.

Grace was tough. She looked as delicate as the orchids that bloomed beside the villa. Slender. Long-legged. The classic beauty of her face, the features that might have been sculpted by a master… It was all deceptive. She could take care of herself. Salim had found that fascinating. How tough she could be in business, how soft she could be in his arms…

In Lipton's arms.

Suppose there was no doubt about what he'd seen in the garden. Suppose it had been real. Suppose Grace had been fighting off a determined predator.

Suppose that predator had been lying in wait for her.

Salim uttered a rough curse. There was only one way to find out.

He went out the door and hurried along the narrow path that led to the hotel. The path was a series of sinuous curves, dramatically lit, enough to see by but not enough to dim the beauty of the night. As he rounded the first curve, a shadowy figure barreled into him.

Grace.

He couldn't see her face but even after all these months, he knew the feel of her, how easily she fit into his arms as he gathered her against him.

She was weeping. And trembling. His arms tightened around her; she buried her face against his shoulder. He could feel her heart pounding against his and he wanted to say something to comfort her but a hot torrent of fury was rising within him, sweeping aside every sane thought he possessed.

Lipton. Lipton! I'll kill you for this!

But that was for later. Now was for Grace. For soothing her. He took a long, deep breath. Concentrated on the moment. Pushed his rage aside and murmured words of comfort as he ran his hand slowly up and down her back.

"It's all right, *habiba*," he whispered. "You're safe now."

She shook her head, sending silken strands of her hair drifting across his lips. Salim closed his eyes, drew her even closer. He held her that way until he felt her heartbeat begin to slow. Then he cupped her face and looked down into her eyes.

"Tell me what happened."

Grace shuddered.

"Was it Lipton?" he said in a dangerous voice.

She shuddered again. It was all the answer he needed. He felt the rage rise up inside him, burning through him like a flame.

"Did he…" He couldn't say the words. "Did he—did he hurt you?"

She shook her head. "He—he didn't get the chance to—to—" Her voice broke. "I fought him and—and—"

Salim's hands slipped up her arms; she made a hissing sound. His rage turned white-hot.

"He *did* hurt you," he said between his teeth.

"My wrist. And my arm. He grabbed it and—and when I tried to get away, he twisted it behind me and—and—"

Salim swung her into his arms and carried her to the villa. He'd left the lights on in the sitting room and as he stepped through the still-open door, he saw that Lipton had done more.

There was a bruise high on Grace's left temple.

His vision blurred. The world turned crimson. For the first time in his life, he understood that "blind with rage" was not just a figure of speech.

He drew a deep breath. Fought for control. Told himself, again, that Grace needed him now. He carried her into the villa's enormous marble bathroom and carefully lowered her into one of the big wicker chairs that faced a glass wall overlooking a private garden.

"Grace." Kneeling before her, he took her hands in his. "You need a doctor."

"I'm—I'm fine."

The hell she was. The bruise on her temple, the marks on her wrist and arm…

"*Habiba.* A doctor—"

"No!" Her eyes pleaded for understanding. "I don't want anyone to see me like this, Salim."

"All right," he said softly. "Then, promise me you'll sit still while I find some aspirin. Will you do that?"

She nodded. That, alone, was indication of her trauma. If there was one thing Grace had never been, it was docile.

Where was a soft facecloth? Aspirin? He yanked open cupboard doors, tossed things out of the vanity. Bath oils. Soaps. All kinds of useless nonsense. Surely there was a first-aid kit in a place that cost three thousand bucks a night.

There it was.

He opened the kit, took out aspirin, poured water into a glass. Told himself to take it easy. He wouldn't do her any good if he let his anger explode.

He squatted in front of her. Held out his palm. Her fingers shook as she took the tablets from his hand. He held the glass to her lips. She drank. She was not simply docile, she was on automatic pilot, and that frightened him as much as anything else.

"Good girl," he said softly. "Just sit here a little longer, okay?"

She looked up at him. "Don't—"

"Don't what?"

Don't leave, Grace almost blurted, but how could she? How could she tell him how terrified she'd been, how all she could think of was finding him, burrowing into the warmth and safety of his arms?

She took an unsteady breath.

"Don't worry about me," she said, and forced a laugh. "I probably look worse than I feel."

Salim rose to his feet. "I'm going to get the ice bucket. Okay? I'm only going into the living room."

So much for not letting him know she didn't want him out of her sight.

"Okay," she said. "Sure. That's fine."

He was back in a moment. "Here we go," he said briskly, dumping the ice in the sink. "Ice. A soft washcloth. Turn your face up to me. That's it." He lifted his hand toward her temple. She flinched and he almost went crazy, but somehow, somehow, he managed to smile reassuringly. "Good. Excellent. Now I'm going to run a cool cloth over your face, *habiba.* Okay?"

She nodded. He was gentle. Still, she made a little sound when he touched her temple.

"I'm sorry," he murmured.

"No, that's all right. You didn't…"

He took her hand in his. The bruises on her arm and wrist were darkening.

"I'm going to flex your wrist," he said, his voice rough. "Only a little, just enough to make sure it isn't broken."

It wasn't, but she caught her breath.

"It's probably strained, *habiba*. Look, I'll phone the hotel. Ask for a doctor who will be discreet and—"

"Don't call anyone. I'm fine."

Salim lifted his head and looked into her eyes. They were clearing; they were hazel again, almost gold, and the look in them was growing determined.

"Grace. This should be X-rayed. Let me just—"

"I said I'm fine."

Salim sat back on his heels, his eyes fixed on her face. "What did he do to you?"

She bent her head. Her tawny hair fell forward around her face, shielding her like a curtain.

"Nothing."

"Damn it, Grace, what did he do?"

She dragged a long breath deep into her lungs.

"He—he said he was weary of playing games. He said I was… He said things. He told me to—to go to the suite and get ready for him. I made it clear that would never happen and—and he got angry."

Salim felt himself growing colder than the ice he'd just used to cool Grace's heated skin. Something ugly twisted in his gut as he rose to his feet.

"Why did you go back to him? Did you think he would simply forget what had happened earlier?"

"I didn't go back to him. I wanted to get my things so I could go to the desk and get a room. I'd reserved one—my secretary did—but when we checked in—"

"You arranged for a room of your own?"

She looked up at him, eyes suddenly lit with fire.

"Of course I did! I tried telling you that in the garden but you wouldn't listen. Do you think I'd actually have agreed to share a suite if I'd had a choice? What kind of woman do you think I am?"

It was an excellent question. The trouble was, he didn't have an answer. She was a thief. She had slept with him so she could steal from him. Could he believe anything she said or did? Could he look past her beauty and figure out what was true?

She was beautiful even now, with a swelling on her temple, her mascara running, her hair a tangle of sun-shot curls. Without thinking, he reached out and stroked some of those curls back from her face.

Her skin felt warm and soft under his touch.

He'd never forgotten the satin of her skin. Of her mouth. The soft, sweet, hot, wild, indescribable essence of her. He had never had a lover like her, had not had one since…

And what did that have to do with anything?

"You should not have gone back to the hotel."

"Thank you for that really helpful advice."

"It was foolish to go back. I told you so."

Her lips curved in a bitter smile. "And you, of course, always know best."

"I know when something is sensible and when it isn't. I warned you he'd try again but you—"

"I told you, I wanted my things. My clothes. My cell phone. But I ran into him in the garden. And—"

"And?"

"And," she said sharply, "I'm tired of explaining myself to you!" Grace rose to her feet. "You were right. I shouldn't have gone back. Is that what you're waiting for me to say?"

"Yes. No. I don't want your thanks, I want—"

To beat Lipton senseless. The realization swept through him with the cold force of an ice storm but he showed none of it. Instead he folded his arms over his chest.

"How did you get away?"

For the first time, a real smile lifted the corners of her mouth. "I kneed him where it did the most good."

Salim grinned. He couldn't help it. That was Grace. A lady and a street fighter in one beautiful package. Add "tough" and "smart" and "honest."

Except, "honest" wasn't a word to use about her. Not anymore.

Salim's grin faded. He moved past her, took a thick terry-cloth robe from the hook behind the door and thrust it at her.

"What's this?"

"What does it look like?" he growled. "Take a

hot bath. Wash the memory of Lipton's hands off you. Then wrap yourself in that robe, order some tea. Better still, order a bottle of brandy. I'll be back by the time you pour the first glass."

"But—where are you going?" She put her hand on his arm. Her touch burned like fire, but how could that be? He'd felt her hand; it was bone-chillingly cold.

"I'll only be a little while."

"Salim. Don't go near him. He's a vicious man. There's no telling what he might do to you."

"Why, *habiba,* I'm touched. You're concerned for my welfare."

Grace snatched her hand away. "Not in the least," she said coldly. "I just wouldn't want you to be laid up and unable to fly me back to California."

"New York," he said, suppressing a rush of elation.

"California," she repeated, and the look on her face was so filled with defiance he wanted to shake her. Or kiss her. Or…

Salim turned on his heel and headed out into the night.

* * *

She wasn't going to do any of the things he'd suggested.

Suggested? Grace laughed. Salim didn't suggest, he commanded. Well, she wasn't taking commands from him. Not ever again. She'd just wait in the sitting room for him to return. After all, that's what sitting rooms were for.

Bad enough she'd had to come running to him for protection but if he thought he was going to order her around, the way he had in the past.....

Oh hell!

She ached. Her arm, her wrist, her head. And she felt soiled. She could still feel the heavy brush of Lipton's fingers over her body.

She stood up, went back to the bathroom, locked the door, turned on the taps in the huge marble tub, checked the basket of luxury toiletries, sniffed at a tiny flask of something called Roses and Moonlight and dumped it into the rushing water. Then she stripped off her clothes, scooped them all up, dumped them in the wastebasket and stepped into the tub. She'd wear the terry-cloth robe to fly in, if she had to. Or something of Salim's. She'd done that once. They'd been caught in the rain and when they reached his place, they'd stripped off their wet things, then showered together. After, he'd wrapped her in a big towel and dried her off, then given her one of his shirts to put on.

Of course, the shirt part hadn't happened that quickly.

First, they'd made love, an inevitable consequence of his drying her off, the touch of the towel giving way to the stroke of his hands, his mouth…

Grace rose so quickly that the water sluiced from her body. She stepped from the tub, grabbed a small bottle of shampoo and to hell with whether it smelled like roses or not, stepped into the stall shower, washed her hair and let the water beat down until her skin was pink. Then she put on the robe—it covered her, as she'd anticipated, from her throat to her toes.

"Ready or not," she told herself softly, and threw open the door.

Salim was standing in the bedroom. His hair was messed. His tie was gone. His shirt was bloodied and there was a small cut beside his mouth. Her heart thudded until she realized he was smiling. That, and her sanity, kept her from flying across the room to him.

"You look," she said with surprising calm, "like a man who just went ten rounds with a gorilla."

He grinned, winced and touched his fingertip to the cut. "One round, and with a pig."

Grace's eyes widened. "What did you do, Salim? I told you—"

"Your suitcase is on the bed." Another grin. "I doubt if you'll approve the way I packed it. Your cell phone is there, too."

"And Lipton?"

"He's breathing, but that aristocratic nose of his has been rearranged." His grin faded. "He'll think twice before he roughs up a woman again."

She knew it wasn't a civilized reaction but knowing that he'd beaten up the man who'd hurt her filled her with pure feminine delight.

"Thank you. For getting my stuff. For—for doing all this for me."

Salim gave her a long, slow look. Her skin was flushed. Her hair hung over her shoulders in long, damp waves. He remembered seeing her like this before, after they'd spent hours making love.

He wanted to take her in his arms and hold her tightly against him.

He wanted to turn his back, walk away and never see her treacherous face again.

How could she affect him like this? He was always in control of his emotions. Always. And he would be, again, once he'd dealt with Grace for the last time.

"I did it for me," he said, his voice gone cold. "You were mine, once. Nobody treats anything that's mine the way that Lipton did."

He saw the swift change in her eyes, the quick shimmer that might have been tears, the tremor of her mouth, but maybe he'd imagined it because now her head was high and she was looking at him the way one of his ancestors had undoubtedly looked at a slave.

"How nice to know you haven't lost perspective," she said, as coolly as he. Then she jerked her head toward her suitcase. "Give me five minutes to dress and I'll be ready."

"For what?" His mouth curved in a wolfish smile. "You want to give me a little reward, *habiba,* you can stay just as you are."

"What I want," she said stiffly, "is to go to San Francisco."

"You mean, New York."

"You're being ridiculous. Haven't things gone your way? You came after me. You confronted me. I get the message. Women don't walk out on you."

"Tell yourself that's what it's all about, if you like, but we both know why I came after you— and why I'm taking you to New York."

Grace opened her mouth, then shut it. Why argue over this now? They had an ocean to cross. There'd be plenty of time to quarrel over his brand of retribution.

"Just get me away from here, okay?"

He nodded. "We'll leave at daylight."

"We'll leave now."

Salim stared at her. Then he began to laugh.

"There's something you need to understand, *habiba*. I make the rules, not you."

"I want to get away from this place as quickly as possible. Can you understand that, or are you really too dense to feel what another human being feels?"

Was that how she saw him? Not that it mattered. He didn't give a damn what she thought about him. Still, it might be wise to leave tonight. For all he knew, she could change her mind by morning.

"Get dressed," he said crisply, "while I shower and change. We'll be out of here in an hour."

She would have said "thank you," but he'd taken out his cell phone and started barking orders into it even as he began undressing. His shirt went first, revealing the broad shoulders, the lightly furred chest, the clearly defined abs she remembered all too well. His hand went to his trousers, undid the buckle, the button above his fly. She heard the hiss of his zipper…

And looked up to see he was no longer talking on the phone. Instead his eyes were on her, as hot and dark as the night that surrounded the villa.

Grace grabbed her suitcase and retreated into the sitting room with as much dignity as a woman in an oversize bathrobe could muster.

CHAPTER FIVE

SALIM looked up from his BlackBerry.

One hour into the flight and Grace had still not said a word. She'd taken a seat after they'd boarded, folded her hands in her lap, turned her face to the window and that was the way she'd remained,

Did she think he'd believe she found the moonless night sky so fascinating?

He grimaced.

The fact was, she probably didn't give a damn what he believed. They were sitting across the aisle from each other but she had wrapped herself in a cocoon of silence.

His steward had asked her what he might bring her. Coffee? Tea? Water? Something to eat, perhaps? She had made the same response to everything, a polite "Nothing, thanks," and after a while the steward had gotten the message.

So had Salim.

What she wanted was to be left alone. She didn't want anything, and she refused to acknowledge his presence. She wore her silence like a sign reading Do Not Disturb.

It might as well have said I Despise You, but that was okay, too.

She could hate him all she liked. It didn't mean a thing. You had to feel some sort of emotion to care if a woman hated you and all he felt for this woman was contempt.

And why would she say anything to him? They had absolutely nothing to talk about. Nothing he'd want to hear because the only topic of possible interest to him would be her admission of guilt and by now, he knew she wasn't about to make one. She was going to keep up the pretense of not knowing why he'd come after her.

Such nonsense. Did she think he'd been born yesterday? He knew what she had done. So did she. Yes, he might get some satisfaction if she confessed and admitted she'd become involved with him so she could gain his trust, slept with him to convince him that all she wanted or needed was him…

He clenched his teeth.

But he was getting his. He'd caught her. And when the plane finally landed in New York, she would pay the price for what she had done. The first thing he'd done after they'd boarded the plane was open his BlackBerry and send an e-mail to the federal investigator who'd been in charge of the case.

Grace Hudson is in my custody. I trust you'll take the appropriate measures when my plane arrives at Kennedy Airport.

He'd added the approximate time of their arrival, said he'd contact the investigator again to confirm it and inserted his signature, the whole thing: Sheikh Salim al Taj, crown prince of the Kingdom of Senahdar, Lion of the Alhandra Desert and Guardian of his Nation, because though the nonsense of it irritated him, it impressed the hell out of some people.

This was one of those times he wanted to impress.

He wanted the Fed and a set of handcuffs waiting on the other end. *Welcome home, habiba,* he'd say, and hand her over with a smile.

Salim glanced at his watch. But that would be a long time from now.

It was midnight; they were somewhere over the Pacific on the start of a flight that would ultimately take more than twenty-four hours to complete, with a refueling stop in Tokyo. Just as on the flight out, a new pilot, copilot and steward would board the plane and relieve Salim's usual crew.

He had instructed his pilot to make the arrangements. He'd wanted no lengthy stopovers on the way east and wanted them even less on the return journey.

The sooner they reached New York and he rid himself of his prisoner, the better. The door would shut on an unpleasant chapter in his life and he could get on with living. Not that he hadn't been living these past few months but...

Hell. What his former mistress had done had turned his life upside down. He'd lived with it for months: his initial disbelief, then his shock, then his mounting rage. And all the inevitable details. The investigation, tracing how she'd accomplished the theft...

Messy, all of it.

But it was over. The thief had been caught.

She would pay for her crime and he would be happy for it. End of story for him. Beginning of story for her. Grace, in prison. Dressed in a shapeless uniform. Living side by side with criminals. But she was one of them. She belonged where she was going.

Yes, indeed. The door would shut on her and he'd forget she'd ever existed.

Salim glanced at her again. She still hadn't moved. Not an inch. Was she thinking about the same thing? The years that stretched ahead of her? The high walls, the iron bars that would be her world?

It was difficult to imagine her in such a setting…

Damn it, so what? What happened to her next had nothing to do with him. She'd brought this down on her own head.

He forced his eyes back to the tiny screen of his BlackBerry. He scrolled through messages, replied to some, made notes about others. He checked the last available stock market figures for Tokyo, London and New York, read the electronic version of the *New York Times* even though he'd done all those things a little while ago. At least it passed the time.

Another hour slipped by. The steward appeared again; he knew Salim's habits on long night flights and he was wheeling a cart that held a coffee service, fruit, cheese and crackers.

"Shall I serve you, sir—and the lady, too, if she wishes—or shall I leave the cart?"

"Leave it," Salim said curtly. The night's events had left him in a sour mood. Grace's silence wasn't helping, even though he told himself it didn't affect him.

He waited until the steward was gone. Then he turned to Grace. *Speak calmly,* he told himself. *She's trying to get under your skin with her sulking so be polite. Show her it hasn't worked.*

"Would you like some coffee?"

No answer. No indication she'd even heard him.

"I said—"

"I heard you. No."

He'd wrung four whole words from her. He suspected that could turn out to be a record for the rest of the flight. And she was still staring out the window.

Salim felt his jaw tighten.. The hell with her. She wanted to do the trip hungry, thirsty and exhausted, so be it.

He drank some coffee. Forced himself to eat something, though the food was like gravel in his mouth. Then he turned his attention to his BlackBerry again.

He could feel his anger growing.

Was her behavior deliberate? Did she think she could elicit his sympathy? Or was her self-imposed silence a sign of her unhappiness? Was it real? Real, he decided. Wonderful. He was bringing a martyr to the stake.

Who could ask for more?

Who could tolerate it for the next twenty-something hours?

"Grace." She didn't move. "We have a long trip ahead of us." Nothing. Not even a twitch. "Are you going to sit there without eating or drinking until we land?" She didn't stir. Salim swore, put the BlackBerry aside and rose to his feet. "I'm talking to you."

Slowly she turned her head and looked up at him. He was stunned. Her face was pale; the bruise on her temple had bloomed like an ugly black and blue flower. Something seemed to turn over inside him. He took the leather chair beside hers.

"You're ill," he said flatly.

"No."

"Of course you are. You look like hell."

"I'm sure I do and thank you for pointing it out."

She started to look away; he cupped her jaw and brought her face back to his.

"I shouldn't have listened to you. I should have insisted you see a physician. You probably have a concussion."

Actually she thought he might be right. It felt like somebody was hammering at her temple. The pain seemed to be growing stronger but she wasn't about to tell that to his Imperial Highness and Inquisitor-in-Chief.

She knew it was ridiculous but agreeing with him would be like granting him a victory and this man had had enough victories at her expense. Worse, he might tell his pilot to turn the plane around and return to Bali. Considering how determined he was to get her to New York, she couldn't imagine he'd do that but with Salim, anything was possible.

Hadn't he proved that all those months back, when he'd capped a week of growing emotional distance by kissing her goodbye and leaving for the coast without telling her what he had in mind? If it hadn't been for her boss, Thomas Shipley, she'd never have known Salim had decided to sweep her out of his life. That he'd already begun the interview process to find her replacement.

Considering how little she'd heard from him that week, he might have spent the time in California finding a replacement for her in bed, as well as in the office.

The memory was still bitter. Just thinking of it now sent a pain knifing through her heart.

"If you get any paler, you'll look like a ghost."

Grace jerked free of his hand. The sudden motion set off a wave of nausea in her belly. It took all her self-control to will it away.

"I have a headache," she said coolly. "It's hardly the end of the world, and why on earth would it matter to you? I'm on your plane. We're heading for New York. My life is in pieces." Her eyes glittered with disdain. "The mighty sheikh won the battle. Don't think I'm foolish enough to imagine you give a damn about the victim."

Victim. Such a clever choice of words, and she

surely figured she had long hours in which to play the role. By the time they landed, she'd look and sound as if he'd physically dragged her across the ocean waves. For all he knew, the media would get wind of what was happening and they'd show up, too. He'd spent his life trying to avoid cameras and microphones but his title and his wealth drew both like magnets, and he knew how they operated.

One look at Grace's bruised face, the smudges of exhaustion already showing darkly under her eyes, the ugly bruise on her temple, and headlines in the *Post,* on TV and in the supermarket tabloids would offer an eager public breathless hints that a cruel sheikh had abused a blond beauty.

No way would he let her get away with that, he told himself grimly, and put his hand against her forehead.

"Don't," she said, and pulled away.

"You're feverish."

"Anger will do that to a person."

Salim rang for the steward. "Aspirin," he commanded.

"I already took aspirin, remember?"

By Ishtar, that snappish tone... He would not take much more of it.

"You took it hours ago. It's time for more."

Grace folded her arms. "I'm not taking more."

"Stop behaving like a prima donna," he growled. "You will do as I tell you."

"You can do your best to ruin my life, Salim, but you can't force me to—"

"Can't I?" he said as the steward delivered a bottle of the tablets, then wisely hurried away. There was a tall pitcher of iced water and glasses on the cart. Salim filled a glass, dropped four aspirin into his palm and extended both tablets and water to Grace. "Your choice, *habiba*. Take the tablets and drink the water on your own or I'll feed them to you."

Furious, frustrated, Grace glared at Salim. Oh, how she hated this man! Those icy eyes. That rigid posture. The determined thrust of his jaw. She knew him well enough to believe every word. She'd seen him turn that steely gaze on opponents at business meetings. He never made a threat he wasn't prepared to carry out.

Besides, aspirin was a brilliant idea. So was water, which might ease her nausea. But you didn't break bread with the enemy...

It's aspirin, idiot! Just take it and shut up.

She snatched the tablets from his palm, tossed them into her mouth, took the glass of water, drank just enough to get the tablets down and shoved the glass at him.

He didn't take it.

"Drink the rest."

"I don't want it. I don't need it. The aspirin went down fine, thank you very much."

"I didn't ask what you wanted, Grace."

"No," she said, "you never did."

Something in her eyes contradicted the sharpness of her tone. Salim frowned.

"And that means…?"

"Nothing. Absolutely nothing," she said, and gulped down the rest of the water. "There. Are you satisfied now?"

He wasn't. He couldn't get the way she'd looked and the words she'd spoken out of his mind. He took the glass from her, set it aside and turned toward her again.

"What didn't I give you that you wanted?" he said, watching her.

"Nothing. Forget I said it."

He thought back to the diamond earrings he'd

given her for her birthday, the antique amber clips for her hair because they were almost the color of her eyes, the little gold boar that dangled from a gold chain he'd bought on impulse when he saw it in a shop window on the Via Maggio during a business trip to Florence.

There'd been other gifts and she'd tried to refuse each one.

I can't accept this, Salim. It's too much, she'd say. And he'd say, *Do it for me, habiba,* and she would smile and tell him he was spoiling her, that she loved whatever it was he'd given her…

Lies, all of it.

She'd played him like a Stradivarius, pretending she wanted nothing from him except his arms, his kisses, and all along she'd been planning to steal a small fortune, steal his honor, steal his foolish belief that she was different from the other women he'd been with who'd wanted everything they could get from him, the jewels from Tiffany, from Harry Winston, from all the pricey shops they name-dropped.

She was different, all right, he thought bitterly.

She hadn't wanted expensive baubles, she'd wanted ten million dollars.

She had turned to the window again. Anger swept through him. He clasped her shoulders and forced her to look at him.

"Answer me, *habiba*. What didn't I give you that you wanted?"

"I didn't say that." Her mouth trembled. "I said, you never asked me what I wanted."

What in hell was she talking about? "It's a little late to tell me you didn't want my gifts, Grace."

She stared at him. Then she made a sound that might have been a laugh.

"You're so dense, Salim! So—so full of yourself. I don't know why I ever thought the thing between us would have worked."

"The thing?" he said, twisting the word with derision. "Is that what you called our relationship?"

"It wasn't a relationship. It was—it was a mistake. I knew who you were. What you were."

"I'm sure you did," he said with a quick, cold grin. "I'm positive you did your homework."

"Has anybody ever told you how arrogant you are, your highness?" Her voice trembled. "Probably not, considering they wanted to keep their heads attached to their necks. Well, let me be the first. You're a self-indulgent, self-centered, insulting, obnoxious, cold-hearted son of a—"

Salim growled, pulled her close and covered her mouth with his. She struggled but he didn't give a damn. It just seemed like the right thing to do. He knew there were other ways to shut her up but she needed kissing right now. Needed to be reminded that she had not always thought of him as such, that when she'd cried out in his arms, taken him deep inside her, ridden him until the world disappeared and nothing existed but the two of them, he had been the heart of her universe.

Suddenly she stopped fighting him.

Her lips softened and clung to his. She whispered his name; he tasted her tears and he groaned, drew her into his lap and kissed her as he'd dreamed of doing all these months, because he had dreamed of it. Of her. He could, at least, be honest with himself.

"Open for me," he said in a husky whisper, and she did. His tongue slipped into her mouth, seeking her heat, her taste. She moaned and her head fell back; he kissed the satiny column of her throat, sought the tender flesh at the juncture of throat and shoulder and nipped her flesh as he had so many times in the past, and she sighed in a way that had always driven him crazy, did it again as his lips moved lower.

Her hand covered his and she moved it to her breast. He could feel the pebbled nipple lifting to his caress through her silk shirt. It pressed against his palm, begging for the heat of his mouth.

"Grace," he whispered, *"habiba..."*

Her hands were in his hair. "Don't talk," she said in a frantic whisper. "Just kiss me. Kiss me. Hold me close and kiss me the way you used to do."

His hands clasped her waist. He turned her so she was straddling him; her skirt rode up on her thighs and he spread his hands over her silky flesh, moved them higher and higher until his thumbs brushed the edges of her panties. She shuddered with excitement; he had grown so hard it was almost painful.

His thumbs slid under her panties. Stroked her. Parted her, gently. She shuddered again and pressed her open mouth to his throat.

"Salim..."

Her whisper almost tore him apart. He knew what she was waiting for. God, so was he! That first caress within her slick folds. The first touch of his fingers against her clitoris.

"Look at me," he said. "I want to see your face when I touch you."

She lifted her head. She was breathing hard; her eyes were blurred. He groaned; he had hardly begun making love to her and yet he was already on the edge.

He'd always loved seeing her like this, lost in passion, in the passion he brought her. Sometimes, he'd prolonged their lovemaking until he was so taut with need he felt as if he were going to explode, until she was begging, pleading for him to end the delicious torment. Watching her in these moments brought such pleasure, the realization that he, only he could strip away the layers of demure sophistication that she wore like a shield, that only he could reach her soul…

Her heart.

He had never forgotten.

He'd lain awake nights, remembering this. The pure ecstasy he'd found with her. And now it was happening again, a spiral of dark passion drawing him down, down, down. Searing his soul, stealing every rational thought from his brain…

Stealing every rational thought from his brain.

Salim froze. How could he be so stupid? This was all an act. She'd wanted something from him and she'd turned on all her seductive power to achieve it. Now she was doing it again only this time, her goal was more valuable than money.

She sought her freedom.

She sighed his name again and he drew back and looked down into her beautiful, traitorous face. Her eyes were on his; she lifted her hand and lay it against his cheek and he thought how easy it would be to carry her to the bedroom at the rear of the cabin and torture her with his kisses and caresses until she pleaded for his possession and then, when she lay beneath him, thighs cradling him, her body hot and open to his, then, as he filled her, he'd tell her what she was doing was useless, that he was still going to turn her over to the authorities but before that happened, he was going to take her again and again, make her pay for the months his arms had been empty and his mind had been filled with rage.

"Damn you," he growled, and shoved her into her seat.

Her face whitened. "Salim?"

"Salim," he mimicked cruelly, "Salim. Is that all you can say, *habiba?*"

"I don't—I don't understand."

"Oh, give me a break, Grace. You understand perfectly." He shot to his feet, angrier than he'd ever been, at her, at himself… Angry and aware of how easily he'd almost fallen into the honeyed trap again.

It wasn't going to happen.

"No," he said coldly, "you don't understand. How can I possibly resist you? That's what you're thinking, isn't it? How could any man resist you?"

She stared at him. If he hadn't known the truth about her, he'd have fallen for the bewilderment in her eyes.

"Come on, sweetheart. Don't go shy on me now. Why not admit the truth and get it over with?"

Tears rose in her eyes. "I was right about you," she said unsteadily. "You're a—a self-serving, arrogant—"

He bent down, clasped the arms of her seat, trapped her with his body and his rage. "Maybe I am, *habiba.*" He moved closer; she turned away and he framed her face with his hands. "At least I'm not a thief like you."

She jerked as if he'd touched a raw nerve. "What?"

"Ah. You don't care for the word." His lips smiled even as his eyes filled with malice. "Does 'embezzler' sound better to your delicate ears?"

The look on her face was priceless. "What are you talking about?"

"I'm talking about you, *habiba.* So many excellent talents in one woman. A mathematical wizard. An actress worthy of kudos." He flashed another smile, one that made Grace's throat constrict. "And, of course, a consummate courtesan. You've always done your best work in bed."

She stared up at him. At the cruel eyes, the terrible smile. Had she ever actually believed she'd cared for this man?

"You're crazy," she whispered.

"I was. Crazy not to have seen through you—but that's the past. What I am now is a man happy to look ahead to the future." His smile vanished; his eyes became icy slits. "You're going to love prison, Grace. And I can't begin to tell you how the thought of you spending years inside one delights me."

"Prison? Prison?" Her voice rose. She pushed her hands against his chest and shot to her feet. "You *are* crazy! I don't give a damn how powerful you are, you can't trump up some kind of lie and send me to prison for it."

"Give it a break, *habiba*. The game's over. You stole ten million dollars of my money, money in my private account, money you knew damned well I used to fund special projects for my people."

"Get away from me, Salim. Turn this plane around. I want to go back to Bali. Steward? Steward! Damn it, you cannot do this!"

"I can do whatever I want," Salim snarled, catching her hands in his. "And what I want, the only thing I've wanted since you ran away from me, is to see you behind bars."

"I didn't run away. I left you. Women are free to do that, shocking as it may be to hear it. Let go of me!"

"You embezzled my money and you ran."

"No. No!" Her voice rose to a shriek and she fought him, fought him like a wildcat but God, her head hurt so badly, so badly…

Lightning sizzled outside the window. The

plane shuddered; lightning lit the night sky again and then…

Bammm!

Everything seemed to stand still.

"Salim?" Grace whispered.

A second explosion rocked the cabin. Tongues of flame streamed past the window. The plane made a sickening lurch, rolled on its side and then they were falling, falling, falling…

The last thing Grace felt were Salim's arms sweeping around her and the weight of his body as he threw her to the floor and fell on top of her.

There was the shriek of the wind, the sound of someone screaming.

And then there was nothing at all.

CHAPTER SIX

WATER. Cold, dark water, rocking him in deadly embrace.

Something sharp, jabbing him in the side. Groans and whispers of metal torn and twisted. Flames, crimson against the night.

Salim shot to consciousness. Gave a wrenching cough. Salt water spewed from his mouth; the acrid stink of jet fuel filled his nostrils.

Where was he? What—

With terrifying speed, he remembered. The plane. The storm. The thunderous roar of the explosions and then the terrifying sight of fire, the sickening sensation of the plane tumbling from the sky…

Grace!

Where was she? He'd flung himself over her as the jet went down, but the impact of it hitting the water must have torn them apart.

He got to his knees. He was in what remained of the cabin. Water was pouring in through the twisted metal. Except for the bursts of light from the fire, it was as black as the bowels of hell.

"Grace," he shouted. "Grace!"

She couldn't be dead. Couldn't be, couldn't be, couldn't—

A moan from behind him. Salim, still on his knees, turned and felt for her in the darkness. Nothing. Damn it, nothing—and then, yes! His hand closed on her wrist.

"Grace," he whispered. She was alive. He wrapped his arms around her and drew her to him, just holding her, feeling the delicate weight of her body against his, the sigh of her breath on his throat. His heartbeat stumbled. "Grace," he said again. She lay limp and unresponsive in his arms. He had no way of knowing how badly she was hurt but he couldn't do anything about it now. He had to get them out of here.

What remained of the plane would go under soon.

The water was already at his waist.

"Hang on," he whispered, even though he knew she couldn't hear him. Holding her close, he made it to the hole in the fuselage. In the dying light of the flames that were consuming the wreckage, he could just make out a sliver of night sky. All the rest was heaving, rushing black seawater.

There was no time to waste. Another few seconds, it would fill the cabin and force it below the waves.

Salim kicked off his shoes, pressed Grace's face against his shoulder, tightened his hold on her and fought his way out into the night. He took a mouthful of water, gagged and spat it out. The ocean was like a living thing, trying to suck him deep into its vast maw, trying to tear Grace from his grasp.

He held her closer. Using only his one free arm, he struck out through waves that seemed as high as a house.

They had to get away before a piece of the sinking plane caught them and took them down with it.

He swam with one arm, Grace clutched against him, for what seemed a very long time. The light from the flames was behind him and he didn't stop, didn't turn around. He shuddered and whispered a quick prayer for the souls of his lost crew.

But he kept moving.

Eventually he could feel the tug of exhaustion. Every muscle was screaming from the impact of the crash. Grace was motionless. He still had no way of seeing what had happened to her. He knew it would be simple to give up. To accept the embrace of the Pacific not as the embrace of an enemy trying to kill him but as that of a lover offering him tranquility.

"No!" Salim shouted the word into the darkness and the roar of the waves. "No," he whispered, and pressed a kiss to Grace's cool cheek.

He would not give up. He was a fighter, he always had been. Maybe a man's life did flash before his eyes in the last minutes of it. Images surely were flashing through his.

He saw the boy he had been, born to a sheikh who had been defeated in bloody civil war, a boy who had grown up in the harshness of the desert. He knew what it was to have an empty belly, to know an almost unquenchable thirst, to shiver in the cold of long desert nights, to have literally fought for his life when his father's enemies had tried to kill him.

And he had survived.

He was strong. He was not afraid of anything. He would come through this and so would Grace. He owed it to her. He had forced her to take this journey. He would not let her pay the ultimate price for his bitter demands.

The waves were high. The wind was fierce. The storm, which had abated, came back with renewed force. Rain beat down on them, lightning sizzled across the black sky.

And in its brilliance he saw…

Something. Something coming toward them.

His heart began to race. A shark? He knew a little about this part of the Pacific; he'd owned a racing yacht for a couple of years, he'd sailed in this piece of the world. The waters were home to more man-eaters than he wanted to think about.

The "something" came closer; the sky lit again and he saw it was a leather cushion from one of the plane's love seats. Salim paddled toward it, made a grab, missed, grabbed again and caught the cushion's edge with his fingertips.

He laughed.

A man, laughing in the middle of a storm in the

middle of a sea so vast it covered a huge section of the earth. Maybe he was losing his mind.

Maybe he'd just found salvation.

"Got you," he said, and tugged the cushion closer.

Grunting with the effort because his muscles were leaden, he eased Grace's arms and torso across it. He must have been too rough because she moaned and despite his exhaustion, his fear, despite everything, he leaned over, cupped her face and kissed her.

"I won't let you die, *habiba*," he whispered hoarsely. "I swear it to you."

The cushion, meant to double as an emergency life preserver, had straps along one surface. Long, agonizing minutes passed as he worked her arms through them. Next he pulled his belt free of its loops, threaded it through one of the straps, secured both their arms to it and knotted the belt so it wouldn't slip.

Finally, exhausted, he hoisted himself up beside her.

The fire had burned out. The wind had died down. The rain had stopped. There was nothing to do now but hang on to the cushion and wait for daylight.

Wait and wonder if his pilot had had time to send out a distress signal.

Salim whispered an ancient prayer of his people into the night. He would keep Grace and himself afloat.

And hope that deliverance came in the form of a search plane and not a hungry shark.

"Thirs'y."

The whisper was soft, born on a breath that stroked his cheek as lightly as a feather. Salim came out of his stupor with a jerk.

"Grace?"

"Thir'sy. So thirs'y…"

She was alive. He almost wept with joy. *They* were alive. They'd made it through the night. On the horizon, dawn streaked the endless dark sky with violet and purple. The seas were still high, lifting them like a giant hand, then dropping them into a trough.

His arm still encircled Grace.

"Thirs'y," she mumbled again, and she parted her lips and turned her face to the sea that lapped hungrily at them…

"No!" He cupped her jaw, turned her face to him. "*Habiba*. I know you're thirsty but you must not drink from the sea."

Grace stared at him. Her face was white; the bruise on her temple was a terrible mingling of black and blue and seemed twice the size it had been.

And there was a terrifying emptiness in her eyes. "Grace?"

She sighed. Her thick lashes dropped to her cheeks. Was she asleep? Unconscious? Salim didn't know, couldn't tell and knew it wouldn't matter as long as they were out here in the middle of nowhere. He couldn't help her while they bobbed like two corks in the pounding water.

He cursed as the sun rose overhead. Soon, it would beat down with a ferocity he knew they could not withstand for long. They drifted. Salim stared in all directions and saw nothing but the endless sea.

Grace slept. After a while, so did he.

He woke with a start.

Something brushed against his foot.

He grunted, shoved Grace higher on the cushion as he kicked out in terror and stared down at the water. There was no telltale fin…

But the color of the sea had gone from the dark blue of the deep to transparent sapphire.

Another soft brush against his foot. He squinted his eyes. Now, he could see tiny flashes of silvery fish swimming through a coral head. Salim caught his breath as he realized what that meant. Coral grew on reefs; reefs surrounded islands. And the water was clear with the crystalline brilliance that accrued to tropical shallows.

"Land," he whispered.

Yes! He could see it. White sand. Green palms.

"Land," he said again, and he laughed with joy. "Grace! *Habiba.* We're going to be all right."

A huge wave dragged them back. Despite the knot he'd made with his belt, the cushion that had saved them was torn away. It vanished in the frothy talons of the ocean. Was the sea toying with them? Had it offered safety only to reclaim them for its own pleasure?

Like a giant playing a child's game, the wave built again. The world seemed to hold its breath. Then, on a throaty roar, the wave tossed them over the reef, into a lagoon, and washed them ashore on a beach of warm, white sand.

And left them there.

Salim didn't move for a long time.

His arm and shoulder seemed locked in place around Grace. His side ached, just as it had right after the crash. His wrist was bloody, his skin abraded where the cushion had been ripped from him.

None of that mattered. All he could think about was Grace. She lay still, unmoving except for the slow rise and fall of her chest.

"Grace," he said softly.

He sat up, wincing at the aches in his muscles and body, and examined her as best he could, his touch gentle, moving her as little as possible. She had injuries; he was sure of it, but he didn't know their extent or even where they were located.

"We're going to be fine," he said, talking to her, to himself, needing the sound of his own voice as reassurance that he wasn't hallucinating. People did that, he knew, when they'd drifted at sea for a while. Maybe the crash hadn't occurred last night. Maybe it had been days ago. No. It had been last night, he was certain, and…

And, why didn't Grace open her eyes?

She had to live. She had to! He couldn't stand it if—if…

It wasn't that she meant anything to him anymore. It was only that he was human. He didn't want to see anyone die. It had nothing to do with Grace, with what his life would be like if she were gone.

She moaned. Quickly he leaned over her.

Wet tendrils of hair were in her face. He brushed them back and caught his breath. Yesterday's bruise was definitely bigger and nastier. A thin trickle of blood oozed from it. She must have slammed her head against something when they crashed.

Carefully he lifted her in his arms, then rose to his feet. There was a tall palm tree not far away. He carried her to it, then eased her down so her back leaned against its trunk.

"I'm going to clean that cut, *habiba*," he said briskly, as if she could hear him. "You just sit there, okay? I'll be right back."

He jogged toward the surf, tearing off his shirt

as he did. He dipped it in the water, rang it out, then ran back up the beach. Grace had not moved. He knelt before her, washed her face with gentle strokes of the wet shirt. She flinched once; he bent and touched his lips to hers, whispered soothing nonsense words, and finished the job.

Better. The blood still seeped from the wound but at least it was free of sand.

Did she have other wounds? He had to find out.

Carefully he undid the buttons of her blouse. It took a long time; it turned out that freeing small buttons from soaking wet silk wasn't an easy task but eventually, he was able to spread the edges of the blouse aside. No wounds or bruises on her throat, her arms, her chest.

A white silk bra concealed her breasts.

Salim reached behind her. Undid the clasp. How many hundreds of times had he done this to her in the past? Undressed her. Undone her bra. Freed her breasts to the touch of his hands, his lips, his tongue.

He forced the thought aside.

He was not her lover. He never would be her lover again. Still, how could he not notice her breasts were as lovely as he'd remembered? High. Round. Small, but not too small.

"They are," she'd once said, "really small."

And he'd smiled, whispered the old saying about wonderful things coming in small packages, and then he'd shown her how beautiful, how sexy her breasts were to him until she'd arched toward him and begged him to do more, more, more…

Salim closed the bra, quickly buttoned the blouse and shot to his feet.

What kind of man would think of such things at a moment like this? What kind of man would think such things about a woman who had deceived him?

Maybe he'd check for injuries later. He couldn't do much about any he might find, when it came down to it, so what was the point?

First things, doable things, first. Reconnoiter. See if the island was inhabited. If it was, they were saved. If it wasn't, he had to find fresh water, something they could eat, shells or stones to make into an SOS sign on the beach, collect dried wood for a signal fire and see if he could remember how to use friction to create a flame.

Could he leave Grace here alone? Hell, what choice did he have? But he didn't want to. Who knew what was waiting for them here? Wild boars. Saltwater crocodiles. Anything was possible.

"Ohhh."

His gaze flew to Grace. He saw her lashes flutter. She was coming to. Quickly he squatted down next to her.

"Grace? Come on, *habiba.* Open your eyes. Come on." He cupped her shoulders. "I know you can do it! Force your eyes open. Look at me."

Her head lolled to the side. Salim drew her toward him.

"Grace! Wake up and look at me."

"Mmm," she whispered and then, slowly, her lashes rose. The tip of her tongue peeped out and slid across her lips.

"My head hurts," she said.

Salim let out a breath he didn't know he'd been holding.

"I'm sure it does. Do you hurt anywhere else?"

She frowned. "Your wrist is bloody. And you have a cut on your side."

He looked down. She was right. The cut was jagged but not deep. His blood and hers had been in the water. Amazing that they'd hadn't become some lucky shark's midnight snack.

"It's nothing. Don't worry about it. Just tell me where you hurt."

Her frown deepened. He could almost see her checking herself for pain. "I ache all over. But my head…" She raised her hand, touched a finger to her temple and winced. Salim grabbed her hand and enfolded it within his.

"You have a bruise there, *habiba,*" he said gently. Hell, he could afford to be gentle with her until she felt better. It wasn't as if it would change anything. She was still who she was but for now, he could show her a little sympathy. "I've cleaned it as best I can. Try not to touch it, okay?"

Grace nodded. "Okay."

The "okay" troubled him. In fact, since she'd regained consciousness, everything about her troubled him. There was a compliancy to her and if there was one word he'd never have used to describe his Grace—not that she was his anymore, but still, he'd never have called her "compliant."

Just the opposite.

His Grace… Damn it, she was Grace. Just

Grace. Grace could be stubborn as a mule, especially if you tried to tell her something about herself. "You don't eat enough," he'd say, and she'd give him a look that said what did he know about it? Or "You're putting in too many late nights at the office," and she'd point out that he was hardly one to comment on late nights. And then there was the time, not long before she ran away, when he told her a condo in his building was for sale. "Suppose I buy it for you?" he'd said, and instead of going into his arms and saying, yes, that would be wonderful, being so near him would be wonderful, she'd looked at him as if he'd said something designed to cause her pain and told him there wasn't a way in the world she'd ever permit him to do that…

And what in hell did that have to do with anything?

Just be grateful she's not giving you a hard time, Salim told himself, and stood up.

"Well," he said briskly, as if he had everything under control, "why don't I scout around? See what's here."

"Okay."

"For all we know, there's a five-star Hilton

with a ten-star restaurant on the other side of this island."

He'd hoped for a smile. What he got instead was another impassive, "Okay."

A chill ran down his spine. He squatted down in front of her again, took her hand, held it tightly in his.

"Grace? Are you sure you're all right?"

"Uh-huh. I told you, my head hurts but except for that—"

"Good. Excellent." And it was, wasn't it? The crash, the night at the mercy of the sea had taken a lot out of her. She was exhausted, that was why she seemed so different. Not compliant. That was the wrong word. She was lacking in spirit, maybe, but if he could find some water, get it into her, follow it with some food, she'd be her old self.

Her old clever self, a sly voice within him whispered. Was it possible her easy demeanor was just a routine to elicit his sympathy? The bruise on her temple was real. That didn't mean anything else was, and how come that was only just dawning on him now?

Salim rose to his feet.

"Fine. That's it," he said, his tone clipped and

cool. "You wait here, I'll check things out. And don't even think about leaving because there's nowhere to go. Do you understand me?"

She nodded. It made him feel like an idiot, making such a stupid speech. They'd survived an experience that could as easily have killed them and here he was, sounding as if they'd landed in the middle of Central Park with a labyrinth of city streets only a brisk stroll away.

The problem was, he was starting to feel as if he'd stepped into another dimension.

"I'll be right back," he said briskly, and set off toward the green wall of palms and scrub. He was almost there when Grace spoke.

"Excuse me…"

Excuse me? Salim wanted to laugh. Instead he took a deep breath and turned toward her.

"Yes?"

"I—I have some questions…?"

He cast an impatient look at the sky. The sun was starting to drop. He didn't have much time to look around before it was completely gone.

"Right. So do I. But questions can wait until—"

"These can't," she said in a breathless rush.

Salim sighed and folded his arms. This was

more like the Grace he knew. She'd never liked putting things off. Neither did he; it was one of the first traits they'd noticed they shared.

"Well? What questions are so urgent they can't wait?"

She hesitated. He saw her throat work as she swallowed.

"For starters… What—what happened? I mean, how did we get here?"

Salim narrowed his eyes. "I don't understand. How did we get here? What is that supposed to mean?"

"Just what I said." She waved her hand at the sand, the sea. "How did we get to this place?"

She didn't remember the night. Well, that was a good thing, wasn't it? Or did she remember it? Was she doing her best to extend her play for his pity?

"You don't remember," he said flatly.

"No."

His gaze locked on hers. "We drifted here."

"Drifted. On a boat?"

The chill danced down his spine again. She was a good actress, but could she really be this good?

"On debris from my plane. We were fortunate

enough that the waves brought it to…" The look on her face stopped him. "What?"

Grace caught her bottom lip between her teeth. "What plane?"

Oh, hell. "*My* plane. The jet that was taking us to the States, remember?"

She stared at him for what seemed forever before shaking her head. "No."

Maybe she was lying. Maybe not. The little he knew about trauma he'd learned, firsthand, during those early years in the desert.

"We were in a plane crash," he said, as calmly as he could. "If you can't remember, don't worry about it. What's important is that we're safe now—and we'll be fine once I do some checking, find us some water and some food." *Maybe, but why add that?*

"Sure."

"Sure" was an improvement over "okay," but not much. Still, he flashed a reassuring smile.

"Be right back," he said again but before he could turn away, Grace spoke.

"One other thing," she said. Her voice seemed to tremble. "Or—or, I guess, two."

Salim sighed. He had no idea how long it would

take him to reconnoiter but he was pretty sure they couldn't afford to waste time if he was right and they'd ended up on an uninhabited dot of land surrounded by thousands of miles of ocean.

"Fire away."

Again, that long hesitation. At last, she cleared her throat.

"The thing is…the thing is, I don't know who you are. I don't know your name. And—and—" Tears began streaming down her cheeks. "And I don't even know mine."

And as Salim's heart began to bang in his ears, Grace covered her face with her hands and her tears became deep, terrible sobs.

CHAPTER SEVEN

SHE looked at the man standing over her through a blur of tears.

He was staring at her as if he thought she'd lost her mind.

Who could argue with that?

A woman whose mind was an absolute blank had certainly lost something.

A rush of blind panic swept through her. What had happened to her? How was it possible not to know your own name, or where you'd been until a few moments ago? And who was he, this tall, broad-shouldered stranger who certainly seemed to know her?

Grace, he kept saying. Was that her name? Why didn't she recognize it? Shouldn't your name feel as if it were part of you? It should. Of course, it should. But each time he called her "Grace" she wanted to look over her shoulder and check to see if someone was standing behind her.

Her throat constricted with terror. Her vision grayed. She couldn't breathe; she began gasping for air.

Instantly the man was on his knees beside her.

"Take a deep breath," he commanded. She did. It was impossible to imagine not doing what he said. "Good. Again. Now put your head down." When she didn't do it fast enough, he put one big hand on the back of her head and gently but firmly did it for her. "Breathe, Grace, or you'll faint. In. Out. That's the way."

The grayness receded. Her lungs filled with air. "Better?"

Better? To find yourself inhabiting a mind and body that didn't belong to you? At least she didn't feel faint anymore; that was something.

"Better," she said.

He sat back on his heels. She could feel him looking at her, his expression questioning and remote. Whoever he was, the fact that her mind was a blank didn't seem to terrify him the way it terrified her. Were they strangers? She'd been in his plane, he'd said. Was he the pilot? Was she a passenger?

"Grace."

She looked up. "Is that my name?"

His eyes narrowed. "Of course it's your name."

"Grace what?"

"Grace Hudson," he said, his eyes still narrowed, as if he was assessing the situation.

"And—and what's your name?" she asked shakily. "Who are you?"

An eternity passed. "I am Salim," he replied.

Salim. Sal—eem. The name suited him. It was strong. Masculine. It was exotic, and there was something exotic about him. His black-as-midnight hair. His olive-toned skin. The high cheekbones, full mouth and square jaw. Her gaze swept over him. He was naked to the waist, his torso, shoulders and arms hard and muscular. Not just strong but with a touch of savagery, she thought, and felt a sudden whisper of unease dance along her skin.

"And—and do we know each other? I mean, if you were the pilot of the plane and I was a passenger, how would we know each other? Except—except, I assume we do, because you know my name, but—"

His expression darkened. "If this is a game, Grace, I don't like it."

"A game?" She gave an astonished laugh. "Why would I want to play a game like this?"

"Because," he said grimly, as he rose to his feet, "it might just suit your purposes."

Grace shook her head and instantly regretted it. Her temple throbbed with pain.

"What purposes? I don't know what you're talking about. I told you, I don't know anything. My name. Yours. I don't know what plane you're talking about, or why I was on it, or why we crashed."

He didn't believe her. She could see it in the way he was watching her.

Anger replaced fear. Did he actually think she'd make up such a story? She hated the coldness in his eyes, hated the way he stood over her, big and gruff and so damned sure of himself that she wanted to scream. Who would want to lie about a thing like this?

And why did he have to stand like that, so that she had to tilt her head back to meet his eyes? It put her at a disadvantage. She knew it. The question was, did he?

She started to rise. The man glowered and motioned her to stay put.

"Stay where you are!"

"Stay where I…?" Grace scrambled to her feet. "Listen, mister, whoever you are, I don't take orders from—"

The world tilted, then swung from side to side. The man cursed, caught her by the shoulders and steadied her.

"Are you determined to pass out, *habiba?* That wouldn't be a good idea. I have things to do before the sun goes down and catering to a drama queen is not one of them."

"I don't need catering to, I need answers!"

"Such as?"

"Such as—such as why were we on a plane? Why did it crash? Where were we going?" Her voice began to shake. "And—and are we the only—the only survivors?"

Was this real? Salim couldn't decide. It was too easy, that she would suddenly come down with amnesia…but her eyes were wide with growing panic and she'd had a blow to her head. Two blows, come to think of it. She could easily have suffered a concussion.

She was trembling. Her face was as pale as the sand.

All right. He'd deal with her as if she actually had forgotten everything. That was the safest thing to do.

"We can talk about this later," he said. "Right now, we need to find water. Night's coming on and I don't want to make things worse than they already are."

"How could things be worse?" Tears glittered in her eyes. "Don't you understand? I don't know who I am!"

Salim looked at her and saw the truth. This was no act. She was frightened and vulnerable and the woman she was at this moment had nothing to do with the woman she'd been until the moment the plane had gone down.

He cursed softly and slid his arms around her.

"Grace," he whispered, "*habiba.* Don't be afraid."

"Don't," she said, but she was speaking to the hard wall of his chest because he'd already drawn her against him. She felt his strength, the heat of his body, inhaled his scent and she let the tears come, let herself sob out her terror and confusion and his arms tightened around her; he rocked her gently, stroked her hair, her back, until, finally she had wept it all out.

He waited until she'd stilled. Then he clasped her shoulders and held her a little way from him. Her nose was red, her eyes were swollen and he hated himself for having been so harsh with her when what she'd needed was comfort.

"I'm sorry," he said. "I shouldn't have doubted you."

"I—I can't understand it. How could I just forget all these things? Who I am. What happened to us. Who you are because you weren't just the pilot, were you? I mean, the pilot of a big plane wouldn't know the names of the passengers."

"It was a private jet, *habiba,* and it belonged to me. You and I were the only passengers." His mouth twisted; his eyes darkened. "There were others. My crew."

"Are they—are they…"

Salim cupped her face. "What matters now is that we survived."

"But why don't I…" She swallowed. "Am I— am I…?" She hesitated, afraid to put a name to whatever was wrong with her. "Am I—you know, am I sick? Do I have some kind of—of mental illness?"

"No," he said quickly. "Nothing like that."

"You mean, I have amnesia?" She wanted to laugh. It was such an awful cliché, the fallback favorite plot device of soap operas and romance novels, and how could she know about soaps and novels without knowing who she was?

He nodded. "It seems that way."

Somehow, his agreement drove it all home. She felt her knees wobble.

"Oh God," she whispered, "God, what am I going to do?"

"You're going to relax. Stay calm. I don't know much about amnesia, but I don't think it generally lasts very long."

"It's lasted too long already," she said, trying her best to make a joke when there was nothing to joke about.

"We'll get through this, *habiba*. Give it a little while and I'll bet everything will come back to you."

"Why do you call me that? *Habiba*. You said my name was Grace. Grace Hudson."

"*Habiba* is—it's just a nickname in my language. It has no real meaning."

Salim half expected his nose to grow. His

words were a lie. *Habiba* meant darling. Beloved. Sweetheart. Once, he had used it because she'd belonged to him. Since finding her yesterday, he'd used it with a full measure of sarcasm. Now—now, he didn't know why he was calling her that, except that it fell easily from his lips.

"And your name is Salim. Salim what?"

Somehow, this didn't seem the time or place to introduce himself by his title. It was the damnedest feeling, all of this; it was as if they'd never met before.

"Salim al Taj." He took her hand and brought it to his lips. "It's very nice to meet you, Grace Hudson."

She smiled, as he'd hoped she would. "It's nice to meet you, too."

A breeze from the sea ruffled her hair. It had dried in a profusion of soft curls around her face. Without thinking, he reached out, let a tawny curl twine lightly around his finger. The rest of her, same as him, was soaked. She was barefoot: he'd sent her shoes to join his on the bottom of the sea during the long night to lessen their weight. The bruise on her temple was a shade of purple he suspected not even Gaughin would have been able to duplicate.

She was not the elegant Grace who had been his mistress in New York, but she was beautiful. Incredibly beautiful. And the way she was smiling at him, no rancor in her expression, no coldness or duplicity….

His heart pained at the memory of what once had been.

He didn't think, didn't plan, he just drew her carefully to him, bent his head and brushed a kiss over her lips.

"You're going to be fine, *habiba*," he whispered and for the first time in months, using the endearment felt exactly right.

Grace didn't want to wait on the beach while he searched the island.

Didn't want to? Salim almost laughed.

She flat-out refused. It was a good thing; he took it as a sign his Grace was back—well, not *his* Grace, not anymore, not that he'd ever think of her that way again, but the Grace he knew had never taken the easy way whether it meant staying inside a restaurant while the doorman flagged a taxi in a downpour or sitting comfortably in his Porsche Carrera GT on a frigid early spring afternoon when the car got a flat during an overnight stay at a Connecticut inn. The tire had blown in a wooded valley; neither his cell phone nor hers would work even when they got out of the car and Salim had said, no problem, he'd change the tire himself.

"You know how to change a tire?" Her tone suggested he'd just told her he knew how to levitate.

He'd grinned, told her he knew how to do lots of things, and she'd snuggled into him and said he was probably all big talk and no action, and he'd said *oh, yeah?* in a way that made her laugh and then she'd gone into his arms and the heat of their kiss had made him go crazy, sliding his hands inside her jacket, under her sweater. Her eyes had darkened and she'd put her hand over his fly—he didn't think he'd ever had an erection as enormous as he did when Grace's hand cupped him as they stood on the shoulder of a New England road on a freezing afternoon.

He'd let go of her with a reluctance he could still feel down deep inside. And she'd stood beside him, watched him change the tire, and when they got to the inn, he'd shut the door to their room and taken her hard and fast against the wall. Then he'd undressed her and taken her to bed and hours later, as they finally lay sated in each other's arms, she'd sighed and kissed his throat while he was still inside her.

And he'd come within a heartbeat of saying…of saying…

"So?"

He blinked. Grace was still standing in front of him, bedraggled, black and blue—and defiant from the tip of her nose to the tips of her toes.

"I am not staying here while you go off and— and get attacked by cannibals!"

This time, he did laugh.

"I'm more likely to be attacked by sand fleas. Look, for all I know, you have a concussion."

"Going with you isn't going to make it worse."

Probably not. And perhaps leaving her alone wasn't a great idea. What he knew about amnesia could be stuffed into a martini olive with room to spare. Who knew what might happen next? Keeping her close so he could watch her might be wise. Besides, they weren't going very far. The sun would set soon, the way it did in the tropics. One moment, the world was bright. The next, it was wrapped in darkness.

He figured they had half an hour, at most.

A tree branch lay in the sand a few feet away. It looked like pine; there were skinny ones of some sort growing among the palms and scrub bordering the beach. The branch was hard and dry. Salim snapped a length off across his knee.

"Stay right behind me," he told Grace. "The scrub's going to be dense. One step in the wrong direction, it could take until morning for me to find you."

She nodded. Her eyes were bright with anticipation.

"Don't worry about me," she said and, damn it, he couldn't help it, he kissed her again. This really was the Grace he knew. The Grace he had—he had become so fond of, but that was way in the past.

A dozen steps took them into the scrub. A few steps more and they were enveloped within a dark green jungle. Salim used his improvised machete to beat back the branches that blocked their way but darkness was settling in here a lot faster than on the beach.

He stopped and turned around. Grace, right on his heels, bumped into him. What had he been thinking, letting her come with him? She was shivering, thanks to her soaked clothes. He had to find a way to get them both dry, find something to eat and drink despite the lateness of the hour.

Palm fronds would make some kind of shelter. As for food and drink… Coconuts! Of course. Palms lined the beach and palms meant coconuts. Why hadn't he thought of that before? And if he couldn't build a fire tonight, he could at least wrap her in his shirt, which he'd wrung out and left spread over a branch. Even if it weren't completely dry by now, it would afford her some protection.

"We can't go any further right now, *habiba*. So here's what we'll do. We'll go back to the beach while we still have a little daylight, find us a coconut, open it and serve up a couple of piña coladas."

He made it sound like a walk in the park even though he knew opening a coconut wasn't going to be easy. He'd opened them years ago, goofing on a Florida beach with his two oldest pals, and it had just been damned lucky that he'd been doing construction work that summer and he'd had a hammer in the trunk of his car, but why worry her with the details?

"Then I'll build us some kind of shelter for the night. We'll go exploring first thing in the morning. How's that sound?"

Not good, Grace thought. Even if they found a coconut, how would they open it? And what good would a shelter do against who knew what might live on this island? Okay, not cannibals but there were other things. Animals. Rats....

"It sounds fine," she said, because even if she didn't know her own name, she knew, instinctively, she wasn't a woman who would waste time complaining about things that couldn't be changed.

Or try to second-guess a man who had gone from distrusting her to kissing her.

Who was this stranger called Salim? He still hadn't explained their relationship. Did they work together? Were they friends? Or were they something more?

She looked up, into his eyes. There was determination there. And courage. And maybe—just maybe, a hint of that something more.

Her heartbeat quickened.

"I'm—I'm glad you're here with me," she whispered, before she could censor her words.

His gaze narrowed. "You mean, you're glad you aren't alone."

She shook her head. "I mean what I said. I'm glad you're here."

A stillness came over him. *He's going to kiss me again,* she thought breathlessly.

But he didn't. He simply touched his hand to her cheek, stepped around her and led the way back to the beach.

His shirt was damp but after he'd buttoned her into it, she wrapped her arms around herself and, a few moments later, she stopped shaking.

"Better?" he said.

She nodded. "But you—aren't you cold?"

"I'm fine," he said briskly. "Come on, now. Let's find those piña coladas."

They didn't find one coconut, they found several. Grace scooped one up and handed it to Salim.

"Now what?"

He hadn't fooled her by making it sound as if this was going to be a snap. Well, why would he have thought he could? This was Grace, not just beautiful but smart.

Smart enough to have used him as a way to embezzle ten millions dollars...

"How will we open this thing?" Grace wrapped her knuckles against the coconut. "It seems pretty tough."

He cleared his throat, forced his thoughts back where they belonged. He always carried a small, antique pocketknife. His father had given it to him when he was a boy; like his watch, it had belonged to his grandfather. Had the sea claimed it? No. It was still in his trousers pocket.

But a knife like this would only be of use after he figured out how to open the coconut.

And then, a few feet away, he saw a piece of twisted metal half-buried in the sand above the tide line. What it was or how it had got there was anyone's guess, but it was worth a try.

Salim went to the jagged lump of metal, took a deep breath, mentally crossed his fingers and brought the coconut down on it...

Whomp!

That put a gash in the husk. Another couple of slams and the brown heart of the coconut was exposed enough to be pried out. One more bang and the nut split open. He snatched it from the ground before the precious milk could leak out and held it toward Grace.

She shook her head. "You did the hard work. You get the first drink."

Salim scowled. "Drink," he commanded.

She did, gulping at the precious liquid before pulling back. "You, too."

He drank, not as much as his dry mouth and throat hungered for, but he pretended he'd had enough and lifted the coconut to Grace's lips again. She put her hands over his, tilted the coconut back and drained it.

"Good girl," he said, and smiled at her.

Was she a woman who liked being called a girl? No, Grace thought, but the way this stranger said it, the word seemed tender, almost intimate.

And he *was* a stranger, to all intents and purposes, despite what he'd told her. Yes, they knew each other. He'd made that clear but *she* didn't know *him*. She knew nothing about him. About their relationship.

Her breath caught.

Were they lovers? Had they been intimate with each other? Would he, tonight, expect her to lie in his arms? Accept his kisses? His caresses? Would he expect to move over her, part her thighs, enter her, fill her, fill her with his heat?

"Grace?"

She blinked. He was staring at her; she tried not to imagine the expression on her face.

"*Habiba.* What's the matter?"

She shook her head. "Nothing. I—I was just—just wondering… You haven't told me what happened to us. Where we were going. Why we crashed."

"Tomorrow," he said, as if he had any real idea of what in hell he'd tell her. *Well, Ms. Hudson, I was taking you back to the States so you could be charged with embezzlement…* "For now, let's see if I can cut some of the meat out of this shell so we can have supper."

It wasn't easy, but he finally did it, first bashing the coconut again and again, then gauging out chunks of it with his knife. It wasn't much of a meal but it brought color back to Grace's face. Maybe this was going to be okay. Maybe, by morning, she'd remember everything. Maybe, by morning, a search plane would find them.

That was what he wanted, wasn't it? Wasn't it?

Salim dragged his gaze from Grace. "Okay," he said briskly, as he cleaned the knife in the sand, then tucked it in his pocket. "Dinner's over. Time to get ready for bed."

It was a bad choice of words. There was no mistaking the pink that crept into her cheeks. He cleared his throat, decided to change the subject.

"How do you feel, *habiba?*"

"Much better."

"No headache? Dizziness? Nausea?"

She shook her head. "Just—just no memory."

Salim silently cursed his stupidity at reminding her of her amnesia. He wanted to take her in his arms and comfort her. She'd done her best to make the words sound light but he could see it was an act.

And she was an excellent actress.

His mouth thinned. He gathered what remained of their meal and tossed it into the sea as he rose to his feet.

"Sleep," he said briskly. "That's what we both need."

* * *

He used palm fronds to make a shelter, leaning them against the trunk of a palm. There wasn't much he could do about the sand on which they'd sleep but he combed through it with his fingers and tossed aside small bits of shell.

It wasn't much, he thought critically, but it would give them some protection against the rain clouds that had been building overhead. They'd surely be rescued tomorrow; whatever he built tonight would be sufficient.

Grace was feeling better; he could tell. She was more lively, there was still color in her face. Again, he wondered if she'd ever really felt ill. If the amnesia was an act.

One more "if" and his head would explode. Not that it mattered. Amnesia or not, she was who she was. She might seem like the Grace he'd known but she wasn't. They would be rescued, they would fly home and he would see to it she was punished for what she'd done to him. No. Not to him. To the integrity of his firm. This wasn't about her leaving him; it never had been.

And none of that mattered tonight.

The sun was kissing the sea when he finished. "Okay," he said briskly, "that's it."

"F—fine."

Salim's brows rose. She was shivering again. Damn, of course she was! With the sun almost gone, a soft breeze coming in from the ocean, the temperature had dropped and his damp shirt was doing nothing to keep her warm.

"Grace." He cleared his throat, busied himself adjusting palm fronds that didn't need adjusting. How to approach this? Hell, there was no way except to go for it. "Grace. Take off your clothes."

Her mouth dropped open. "What?"

"You're still wet. So am I. The sun's gone, the wind's up… The only way we can get warm is to get rid of our wet clothes."

Grace stared at him. Take off her clothes? "But," she said, "but—"

"You want pneumonia on top of amnesia?" he said grimly. "Don't be stupid, Grace. Take off your clothes."

He was right. She knew he was right. She was cold. Terribly cold, right to the marrow of her bones. How could that be? This was a tropical island. This was…

Her heartbeat stuttered.

He was getting undressed with his back to her. His trousers. His socks. His hands went to his boxers and her heart all but slammed into her throat. To her relief, he hesitated, gave a barely perceptible shake of his head and turned toward her.

"Leave on your underwear, if you wish."

His voice was hoarse. Grace suspected she had no voice at all. He was, in a word, magnificent. Those wide shoulders, strong neck and powerful chest were more than matched by his washboard belly.

Her eyes skimmed the rest of him.

Narrow hips. Long, well-muscled legs. And then there were those boxers…those boxers, and the sudden tenting of the fly…

Her gaze flew to his.

"I'm human, *habiba*," he growled. "Look at me like that, you cannot expect me not to react."

Grace ran her tongue over suddenly dry lips. I don't—I can't—"

"Do you need my help?" His voice turned low and husky. "I'll undress you, *habiba,* if that's what you prefer."

Her cheeks turned the deep pink of the last

rays of the sun as it dipped into the sea. She turned her back to him, pulled off her blouse, her linen skirt, told herself they were really wearing as much as they would if they'd come to this beach to swim…

She took a deep, deep breath. Then, head high, she swung toward him. He was lying on the sand, on his side, and—*thank you, God*—it was already too dark to see the expression on his face.

"This is about staying warm, *habiba*, nothing more."

She crossed the distance between them quickly, lay down at least a foot away. The night had become a black silk cloak shot with millions of stars. The surf lapped gently at the sand; somewhere in the scrub, a bird gave a soft peep.

A tremor went through her. She was cold. Or she was something else, something she didn't want to name. Another tremor racked her, and another…

"By Ishtar," Salim said, "stop being such a little fool!"

He wrapped a warm, powerful arm around her. Drew her back against him. Draped one leg over hers. She felt the heat of his body curved around hers. The soft whisper of his breath on her neck. Heard his breathing slow.

He was asleep. It infuriated her. She would lie awake all night. How could she sleep wrapped in his embrace? Feeling the beat of his heart against her back? Feeling him holding her as if they were lovers.

Feeling as if nothing could ever harm her, as long as she was in his arms.

Grace yawned.

And tumbled into sleep.

CHAPTER EIGHT

SOMETHING soft was tickling Salim's nose.

Still locked in sleep, he tried to brush it away. *"Mmmf,"* he grumbled, brushed at it again...

And came awake to the brightness of morning. The hiss of the surf. The hot sun in a cloudless sky. The blue ocean, white sand, overhanging palm fronds...

And Grace, asleep in his arms.

The feathery whisper of her hair against his face was what had awakened him. She was facing him, curled against his body, her face buried against his shoulder. Her hand lay over his heart and he could feel the gentle warmth of her breath against his naked chest.

It was how they'd always slept, after making love.

He remembered the comfort and closeness of

holding her after hours of passion, the sweetness of waking to find her in his arms. There had been nights he'd lingered until almost dawn, not wanting to leave her, knowing he had to because spending the entire night in her bed was not a good policy. That she'd reach out to him in her sleep, murmuring that she didn't want him to go, made it even harder to do...

Even as it assured him that he was doing what had to be done.

Women were nesters, even the few who were hotly determined to climb to the top of the corporate ladder, like Grace. A man slept with a woman night after night—actually slept with her—their relationship might take on a hint of domestication.

And that had never been what he'd wanted.

Sex. Companionship. An evening out, incredible sex, a last kiss and a taxi home well before dawn. He had no time in his life for anything even resembling commitment, no desire for it, either. He wasn't sure he'd ever change his mind about that but it would not present a problem. Yes, a crown prince needed a wife and heirs; he would eventually have both, but his marriage would be a necessity of state, not a calling of the heart.

Salim didn't believe in the heart as anything but an organ that pumped blood through one's body.

His father believed the same. He had divorced his first wife when she'd proved infertile. He'd taken another who had borne him Salim. Duty accomplished, she'd kept her title and the fortune Salim's father had given her and moved on. Now, the woman who had given birth to Salim divided her time between England and America; he had not seen her since he was a boy but he had never missed her.

Royal marriages were based on duty, not emotion. Relationships outside of marriage were based on sexual fulfillment. He had always understood that.

Western women, for the most part, were the ones who couldn't grasp the concept.

Still, there'd been times he hadn't wanted to leave Grace's bed. He was a man in his sexual prime. She was a sensual, passionately responsive woman. Wanting to stay the night with her in his arms had to do with basic instincts.

It couldn't have been for anything else, he

thought, closing his eyes as he drew her even closer.

He wanted to stay where he was right now, too. No surprise there. The crash. The hours drifting at sea. Finding themselves on an island that seemed to be in the middle of nowhere. The ache in his muscles, the burn of the cut on his side…

Staying here was a lot better than getting up and starting the search for food and water.

And the woman in his arms needed sleep. She'd been through one hell of an ordeal. The experience was far worse for her. Grace had obviously never known anything but luxury. The best schools. Wealthy, caring parents… They'd never talked about their childhoods but her elegance and intellect spoke for themselves. Life would surely not have prepared her for anything even close to this.

Or for a man like him.

He could only imagine her horror if she had known he'd once worn rags, not five thousand dollar suits; lived in a tent, not a penthouse; been charged with tending his father's Arabian horses, not an investment empire worth billions.

Not that it mattered.

She had no need to know any of that. She'd been his mistress and now she was his embezzler. That she seemed to have amnesia didn't change a thing.

It was just that he didn't know what lay ahead. They would need to be strong, which was why he was willing to let Grace sleep a little longer. He might wake her, if he took his arm from under her shoulders. The right thing to do was to lie here a few more minutes.

Or perhaps to thread his hand into her hair, see all that tawny silk tumble though his fingers. Just like that. And put his lips to her forehead again, to check for fever, just like that. Or to see if her skin really did feel like silk under the whisper of his kisses. Here. And here. And here, on her slightly parted lips. A tremor went through him as he felt the softness of her breath, mingling with his.

"Salim."

His name sighed from her lips. She had said it last night, when he'd "introduced" himself to her. Now, she whispered it as she had months ago. It brought a rush of memories, and he groaned and kissed her again.

Her eyes opened. They were blurry with sleep, and then with desire. Her mouth curved against his and she brought her hand to the back of his head, her fingers gently tunneling into his hair, bringing him closer to her.

The delicate tip of her tongue touched the seam of his lips and he groaned again and accepted the sweet offering by hungrily returning the pleasure.

This was the way she'd always greeted his morning kiss because yes, despite everything, he'd eventually begun to spend an occasional night in her bed. He'd used the weather as an excuse, the lateness of the hour but the truth was, he hadn't wanted to leave. He'd wanted to awaken with her in his arms; kiss her awake with tender, teasing kisses and then the tenderness would change, their bodies would catch flame and Grace would raise herself to him, whisper his name.

He had been so long without the taste of her, the warmth, the sighs that told him she wanted him…

He knew there were reasons not to do this but right now, it didn't matter. This—the heat of her mouth, the fragrance of her hair, the feel of her against him—this was what mattered. Nothing else.

He could feel her growing softly pliable in his arms. And feel himself hardening. He was fully, almost painfully erect; he felt as if all the blood in his body had collected in the powerful length of his penis.

Grace felt it, too. She gave a little gasp and he slid one hand down her spine, cupped her bottom, lifted her into him. She gasped again and he, God, he almost came. He was pressed hard against her, only the thinness of his boxers and her panties separated flesh from flesh.

She put her face against his throat. He could feel her trembling as he moved against her, as she arched against him.

He slipped his hand inside the leg of her panties. She gasped; he felt his heart pounding. Her bottom was cool and delicately curved; it fit his palm as if this was what his palm had been made for. Gently he moved his hand, felt the first soft brush of her feminine curls against his fingers.

A shudder went through her. Or through him. He didn't know which, didn't know where she ended and he began. It had always been like this, from their first time together, a connection so sweet, so powerful it had made him tremble.

"Salim…"

She whispered his name. He caught the whisper with his kiss.

"Habiba," he said softly, and rolled her onto her back.

She gasped as his thumb swept over the juncture of thigh and torso. Swept over the tender flesh again, closer and closer to the prize he sought. His breath caught; he felt the dampness, the honey her womb created for him, only for him…

"Salim." Her voice was raw; she put her hands against his chest. "Stop."

He heard the word but it didn't make sense. He was lost in a world of sensation, on the brink of feeding a hunger he had been unable to assuage in the months since she'd left him.

"Salim! Stop it."

The edge of panic in her voice brought him back. His eyes cleared; he saw Grace looking up at him, white-faced.

"We can't do this."

"I want you, *habiba*. And you want me."

"No!" She shoved against his chest. "I don't want you. Not like this."

He grinned. "I'm open to suggestions."

Her eyes snapped with anger. "Get off me! I don't know you! I don't know me! I'm not going to—to make love when you and I are strangers."

Strangers? What a joke. "We aren't strangers," he growled.

"What are we, then?"

What, indeed? The answer came within a heartbeat. He was a man who'd had his honor stolen from him, and Grace was the woman who had stolen it.

Salim rolled away, got to his feet and began dressing. His clothes were stiff with salt but dry. "How is your head?"

"It hurts."

"A lot? A little?"

"Salim…"

"If you're feeling up to it, we have to get moving."

"Salim. Answer the question."

"The sun's been up for hours," he said brusquely, "and we have a lot to do."

"Why won't you explain?"

He heard the shifting of the sand as she sat up behind him. He could imagine the way her hair would be tumbled over her shoulders, the soft color his kisses had brought to her lips.

"What is there to explain? That Hilton you're hoping for. We have to get started if we're going to find it."

"Not that." She paused. "I was talking about—about—"

About what had just happened between them. About what he'd said, that they weren't strangers. He turned and looked at her. She looked just as he'd imagined, only more beautiful. Somehow, that made his anger harden.

"I know what you're talking about," he said, deliberately choosing to misunderstand her. "A man often wakes with an erection. If a woman's available, that adds to it."

It was a crude thing to say. Anger at himself for forgetting what she was made him speak with the specific intent of putting things in perspective. Still, he felt a second of regret when her face whitened.

Her recovery, though, was quick.

"I am not available," she said. "And thank you for explaining that that was an erection. I really couldn't tell."

It was vintage Grace. She'd always been quick and sharp and witty.

He thought about going back to her, flinging her down on the sand, clasping her wrist high over her head and showing her exactly what this was all about but for all he knew, that would play right into her hands.

Instead he scooped up her blouse and skirt and tossed them to her.

"Get dressed. And make it quick, or I'll tell the cannibals to come and get you."

She called him a name. It was an imaginative one and he was glad she couldn't see him grin as he headed for their little cache of coconuts so he could choose one for their breakfast.

He had the feeling it was going to be a very long day.

He spent a few minutes checking things out.

The cut in his side was a minor injury. Still no sign of infection, though it made him wince to clean it. Grace acted as if she didn't hear him when he told her to sit down on a tree stump and let him take a look at her temple so he grabbed her wrist, plopped her on the stump, cupped her face with his hands and took a long, hard look at her forehead. The swelling had gone down but the color was still spectacular.

He held up three fingers. "How many?" he said briskly.

Her look was filled with disdain. "Three."

He switched to five. "Now how many?"

"Five."

"Any vision problems at all? Do you see spots or anything else you shouldn't?"

Her smile glittered. "Just you," she said, so sweetly that he had to hide another grin.

"Okay, then. Let's get moving. If you can't keep up, let me know."

"Keep up with you?" She snorted as she fell in behind him. "I was a Girl Scout..."

He heard her breath catch; he swung around and looked at her. "What's the matter?"

"I was a Girl Scout," she said in small voice. "How do I know that?

Salim's eyes narrowed. "What else do you remember?"

"Nothing. Only that I was a Scout. I didn't have a regular uniform, just the hat and scarf because the whole thing cost too much..."

Grace? Without something because of its cost?

"I hate this," she whispered. "It doesn't make sense. Not remembering anything and all of a sudden, I could—I could see me, a little kid on a hiking trail…and now it's all gone, I can't see anything, can't see me, can't see—"

Salim closed the short distance between them and wrapped his arms around her. She was shaking and he cursed under his breath and gathered her close.

Her amnesia was real. He was finally convinced of it. It didn't change the basic facts about her or what she had done but for now, she wasn't the same Grace she had once been.

She was the Grace he'd lost his head over.

But that would never happen again.

If they'd been scouting a location for a movie about castaways on a tropical island, this place would have been the hands-down winner.

The bright daylight helped Salim find what he suspected was a game trail through the scrub. A good thing. Sand covered with tromped-down vegetation was a lot easier on bare feet. Eventually the scrub gave way to a forest of palms, pines and flowering shrubs. Pink and white orchids grew everywhere; vines that bore flowers in vivid shades of crimson and gold twined around tree branches. Birds with brilliant plumage darted overhead and once, they startled a tiny deer on the trail ahead of them.

Salim's stomach growled in acknowledgment.

Definitely, this was a game trail. There was food here, though it was on the hoof, and he'd have to figure a way to trap it. Grace's soft cry of delight at the sight of the animal told him that where he saw venison, she saw Bambi, but he'd deal with that when the time came.

And they found water, a swift-running stream that tumbled through a rocky bed. They both threw themselves down on the mossy bank, lowered their faces and drank their fill.

Grace sat up first, laughing with delight.

"Did you ever taste anything so wonderful?"

Salim looked at her. Water dripped from her lashes and face; her blouse was torn and there was dirt on the tip of her nose. He had never seen her look more beautiful…and, yes, he had tasted something even more delicious than the long-sought water.

Grace's mouth. Her skin. Her nipples…and damn it, what was wrong with him? He was trapped on an island with what he suspected was little chance of escape and instead of coming up with clever ideas, his head was full of images so hot they left him feeling scorched.

He wiped the back of his hand over his mouth and stood up.

"This is no time to sit around talking," he said sharply. "I'd like to get a couple more hours of walking done before we start looking for a place to spend the night."

Her smile disappeared. "You're right," she said, and she rose to her feet and fell in behind him again.

Salim figured they'd begun their trek at maybe eight in the morning.

It was an hour or so past noon now, judging by the angle of the sun. His entire body ached, his feet worst of all. The game trail had started to fade. There were leaves underfoot but there were also twigs and stones, and without shoes each was an enemy.

He stopped several times to ask Grace how she

was doing. It had to be as difficult for her as for him. More. Her feet were small and narrow. Delicate. She'd surely feel every impediment along the path but if she didn't want to admit it, he wasn't going to press her…

Until he heard a soft cry behind him.

He swung around and found Grace sitting in the middle of the trail, clutching her left foot.

"What happened?" he said as he dropped down next to her.

"I stepped on something… Ouch!"

"Here?"

He pressed lightly against the ball of her foot and she jumped.

"Yes, there. Damn it, Salim—"

"Grace," he said mildly, "how about a little cooperation? I'm trying to see what… It's a thorn."

"A thorn," she said wearily. "Well, pull it out."

"Not until I get a better look. If it's barbed, I'll want to cut it out."

"You just love that little knife of yours."

He grinned. She was trying to keep up her spirits and he couldn't fault her for that.

"I think there's a clearing ahead. See? There's sunlight coming through those trees."

She nodded. "Find me a branch. I'll hobble on one foot until— Hey. Hey! Put me down."

"When we get to the clearing."

"I am perfectly capable of walking."

"And perfectly capable of stumbling and driving that thorn deeper. Stop complaining, *habiba,* and enjoy the ride."

How could she enjoy the ride?

What woman would want to be snatched up in a man's arms and carried off like a trophy of war? Especially if it were this man. So big. So sure of himself. So coldly arrogant.

So sexy.

God, so sexy.

Grace's face heated, just thinking about what had happened this morning. Awakening in Salim's arms. His body pressed to hers, his erection massive and hard against her belly. She'd disparaged it only because the man needed taking down but, oh, the feel of it against her...

Then he'd kissed her. Touched her. Slid his big, hot hand under her panties as if he had the right to do it but then, he did everything like that, as if he had a prince's privilege to take whatever he wanted.

A prince's privilege. Why had those words come to mind?

It didn't matter.

Their relationship did.

Had he done whatever he'd wanted with her in the past? They weren't strangers, he'd said, but he hadn't explained what that meant. She couldn't figure it out from the way he dealt with her, sometimes with a passion that scalded her, other times with an iciness that was frightening, and sometimes— like now—with a tenderness made all the more appealing by his potent masculinity.

And what kind of name was Salim? Not American. She didn't know her own name but that didn't mean there weren't names in her head. John. Arthur. Steven. All kinds of names, but Salim…?

"I know you don't want to do it, *habiba,* but it would help if you set aside your pride and put your arms around my neck."

Grace blinked. She'd tried to keep her distance. Stupid, when you considered one of his arms was looped under her knees and the other was around her hips.

Gingerly she did as he'd asked.

"Thank you," he said, his voice tinged with sarcasm. "Your sacrifice is much appreciated."

"You're welcome," she said, trying for the same tone but not quite making it because, somehow, holding on to him made this more intimate. And she didn't want any intimacy with Salim, whomever he was. Well, yeah, she did—and that was the problem. Why was she so responsive to him? Why did everything about their dealings with each other seem so explosive?

"Salim. You have to tell me who you are. Who *we* are. How we know each other and…ohhh!"

Ohhh, indeed. Salim stumbled to a halt as they stepped out of the forest.

They were in a meadow, lushly carpeted in deep, dark green grass. Majestic banyan trees reached to the sky, standing on knuckled roots that looked as if they had been there since the start of time. And straight ahead, glittering like a spill of diamonds, a waterfall tumbled fifty feet into a pool of sapphire-blue.

"Hold on tight, *habiba*," Salim said, his voice filled with laughter, and he set off at a trot for the pool and the frothing water plummeting into it.

Icy droplets danced over their skin as they

drew close; the roar of the water filled the air. Salim thought he'd heard some kind of dull roar the last few hundred yards in the forest but the heavy foliage had absorbed the sound and he'd assumed they were nearing the ocean.

Instead they'd stumbled on this.

It wasn't a five-star Hilton or even a cabin. It wasn't a plane or a helicopter. It was only a waterfall but one so spectacular, so beautiful that, for the moment, it was enough to make him forget the terrible reality of their situation.

He began to laugh. So did Grace. *Oh, Salim,* she kept saying, *oh, isn't it wonderful?*

It was. It was brilliant. He turned her so she was facing him, held her by the hips with her feet off the ground, danced with her, whirled her in circles while she looked down into his eyes and laughed with him…

Until their laughter stopped and he cupped one hand behind her head and brought her mouth to his for a deep, hungry kiss.

Her lips melted beneath his. There was no other way to describe it. Her lips, all of her, melted. She dug her hands into his hair, opened her mouth, touched the tip of her tongue to his and when he growled and held her even closer, she slid down his body, down, down, her breasts soft against his chest, her belly flat against his…

"Ahh!"

Her soft cry of pain shot him back to reality. Her foot. The thorn. What kind of man let sexual need blank his mind to everything else?

"Easy," he murmured as he carried her to the water's edge and sat her gently on a moss-topped boulder. He knelt before her, lifted her foot onto his knee and bent over it. The thorn had not gone any deeper and it wasn't barbed. Salim took out his knife and used one blade and his thumb to ensure he withdrew the thorn without snapping it in half and inadvertently leaving the rest embedded in her flesh.

When he was done, he held up the knife, the thorn a dark line against it.

"The operation was a success," he said, smiling.

Grace smiled back at him. It was the smile she used to give him, one that said, more clearly than words, "I love everything you do to me." He hadn't seen that special smile in a long time, not just since she'd left him but before that, while she was still his mistress.

That smile, and its power to make his heart lift, had vanished before she had.

How come he hadn't realized it until now?

Had that smile gone because she'd been getting close enough to him to gain access to the computer codes he kept in a leather-bound notebook in his study? Or…was it possible there'd been some other reason? Hadn't he made her happy back then?

"Grace," he whispered, and drew her toward him.

She fit into his arms perfectly. When he stood and brought her to her feet, her eyes locked to his, her hands on his chest. He could drown in that look. In the feel of her. The scent of her skin.

Slowly he undressed her. Her torn blouse fluttered to the grass; she put a hand lightly on his arm and lifted one foot, then the other as he unzipped her skirt and slid it down her body.

Her hands went to his shirt and she undid the buttons. Her fingers trembled; there was such an expression of innocence and desire on her lovely face that he caught her hands in his and kissed them before he let her push his shirt back on his shoulders.

"My turn now," he said thickly, loving the way

her head fell back when he reached behind her and undid the clasp of her bra. Her breasts, as beautiful as he'd always remembered them, tumbled into his hands. She moaned and he caught his breath at the feel of them. The sight. Their satiny smoothness. The blush of her nipples.

He watched her face as he feathered his fingertips over those delicate buds. What he saw in her eyes turned him harder than he'd thought possible. She cried out and he bent to her, nuzzled the valley between her breasts, kissed his way to one beaded tip before drawing it between his lips.

Her knees buckled.

He caught her in his arms. Carried her to the nearest banyan tree, lay her down in the shade of its massive, leafed branches and she thought, *This is wrong, it's wrong, I don't know this man, I don't know anything about him...*

But she did.

Somewhere deep in her heart, in her soul, she knew him. Knew the feel of him, the taste of him, knew that he was a part of her, that she was a part of him...

"Salim," she whispered.

He lowered his head and kissed her. "I'm here, *habiba*. Tell me what I ache to hear. Say that you want me."

Her smile was that of the siren mythology said had lured ancient sailors to exquisite doom.

"I want you," she sighed, "Salim, I want you, want you, want—"

He kissed her to silence, closing his mouth over hers, rolling over with her in the grass, his hand slipping down her silken belly, inside her panties, down and down until he cupped her and she cried out and bucked against his questing fingers, and the roar of the waterfall was almost as loud as the roar in his head…

Except, it wasn't the waterfall he heard.

It was a white Jeep with a pink and white striped canopy, racing along the grass toward them.

CHAPTER NINE

AT FIRST, Grace was so stunned by the unexpected sight that she froze.

Then she realized she was almost naked, lying in Salim's arms as a vehicle barreled toward them.

"Oh my God," she whispered, "Salim—"

He sat up, shielding her with his body, grabbed for his shirt and wrapped it around her shoulders. She stuffed her hands through the sleeves. There was no time to reach for more than that; the Jeep was braking only a few yards away.

Salim got to his feet, held his hand out and drew her up beside him. His shirt was in tatters but it hung to her thighs. She probably looked like a woman who'd been doing exactly what she *had* been doing, she thought, frantically running her hands through her tousled hair, but at least she was covered.

"Stay behind me," Salim commanded.

Grace slipped behind him. What was there about the unexpected sight of another human being when you thought you were alone on an isolated island in the middle of the Pacific that was so terrifying? She had ridden the New York City subways at night, lived in a fifth floor walk-up in an ungentrified part of lower Manhattan when she was just starting out, and her heart had never pounded like this…

And how did she know all that?

Never mind. Now wasn't the time to figure it out. The only sure thing was that her knees were like jelly and she was filled with gratitude that Salim was with her and would handle this.

A man stepped from the Jeep. He was big and bulky; he wore beat-up jeans, equally beat-up sneakers and a T-shirt that told the world that Beer Says It Best.

Said what best? Grace thought, and shuddered at the possibilities.

Unknowingly her hands crept to the back pockets of Salim's trousers. She curled her fingers into the fabric and pressed as close to him as she could manage.

"It will be all right, *habiba,*" he murmured. "I would never let anything happen to you."

She knew he meant it and leaned her forehead against his back. She could feel the tension in his body. He was a tiger, ready to spring to protect that which was his.

Was she his? Was he hers? Suddenly it seemed so right to stand close to him, to lean on him, to believe he would give his life for her if it came to that. She knew she'd felt this way before, with Salim. The stunning sense of closeness. The oneness. The same emotions that had flooded her senses when he'd begun to make love to her…

"Who are you?" Salim said as the man drew nearer.

"I have a better question, mate. *Who* are *you?* And what in bloody hell are you doing here? This is a private island."

Private for what? Was it home to a hospital for the criminally insane? Were there terrible experiments taking place in underground chambers? Every bad movie she'd ever seen raced through Grace's mind.

"I am Salim al Taj."

"Don't mean a thing to me, mate. You'd better have a damned good story."

She felt Salim take a deep breath. "I am Sheikh Salim al Taj," he said coolly, "Crown prince of the Kingdom of Senahdar, and I want to know your name and the name of this place."

The shocked expression on the man's face surely mirrored Grace's own. A sheikh? A prince? The stranger she'd almost made love with was royalty? A jolt of unreasoning anger flashed through her. Why hadn't he told her that?

The man's brows rose. "Are you a friend of Sir Edward's, then?"

"Who?"

"Sir Edward Brompton. The bloke who owns this island."

Grace could actually feel the tension flow from Salim's muscles.

"Brompton?" he said. "Of Brompton Shipping? Then, this must be Dilarang Island."

"It is. You here at his invitation?"

Salim laughed, reached back and drew Grace forward. He kept his arm around her as he gathered her close against his side.

"I wish we were, Mr...."

"Name's Jack. But if Sir Edward didn't invite you—" He seemed to notice their beat-up clothes for the first time. "Blimey! What happened to you two?"

"Our plane went down in the storm night before last." Salim's voice roughened; Grace felt his arm tighten around her. "Miss Hudson and I were the only survivors."

Jack nodded. "Sorry to hear it, but glad the two of you made it," he said, acknowledging Grace's presence with a smile that transformed him from pirate to charmer. "Hell of a storm, that. Took out our power. Still trying to get it back up."

"No power. How about satellite?"

"Lost that, too. Don't know why."

Grace moistened her lips with the tip of her tongue. "Then, there's no way to contact anybody and get help?"

"Not yet, miss, but I promise we have everything else you could possibly need." He strode toward them, grinning, hand outstretched to Salim. "Welcome to Dilarang."

Everything they could possibly need?

Grace almost laughed at that description. The

house on Dilarang Island—Forbidden Island, Jack told them with a grin—surely contained everything anyone could possibly need or want in a dozen lifetimes.

And calling it a "house" was a misnomer. It was a mansion, and stood on a rise a ten-minute ride beyond the waterfall.

"Ten minutes by Jeep," Jack said cheerfully, "half a day if you'd kept going on foot. The forest picks up again just beyond that meadow."

Surrounded by gardens of red, pink and purple foliage, shaded by tall palms and trees laced with wild orchids, the mansion overlooked a white sand beach kissed by the sapphire-blue waters of the South Pacific.

The structure itself was a contemporary sprawl of glass, stone and teak, highlighted by graceful touches that hinted at the Balinese culture. Rooms opened onto rooms, all with breathtaking views of the forest or the sea. Ceilings soared toward the sky; massive stone fireplaces stood ready to chase the chill of an occasional cool night. There were, by Grace's quick count, at least a dozen bedrooms and baths.

"There's a full staff and they'll be happy to see

to your every need," Jack said. "Sir Edward's not here, I'm afraid, not expected for weeks, actually, but I know he would want you to make yourselves completely at home." Another charming grin. "A kind of 'his castle is your castle' thing, I'm sure, Sheikh Salim."

Salim smiled. "Thank you. And I'd appreciate it if you'd let me know when you reestablish contact with the outside world. I've no idea if my pilot managed to get out an SOS, but as soon as my people realize I'm missing…"

"Of course, sir. One of our chaps is a whiz with computers and such—he's working on the problem now. Meanwhile, I'll have the chef put together something for you to eat while you clean up. There's clothing in every bedroom— Sir Edward's guests can simply take their pick. Your choice of bedrooms, of course, though I'm sure he'd want you to have the master suite."

"Oh," Grace said, "but we'll need—"

"Sounds perfect," Salim said, before she could finish the sentence.

Moments later, they were alone in a high-ceilinged bedroom dominated by a vast, four-poster bed hung with yards and yards of ivory voile. A five-bladed teak ceiling fan turned lazily overhead. The bed itself faced a wall of glass; the French doors set into it were open to a huge private terrace and, beyond it, a glittering infinity pool and then the sea.

"I was going to tell Jack that—"

"That we would need two bedrooms." Salim nodded. "I know. But until we're sure of things, I think it's wise we stay together."

He looked so serious that Grace couldn't fault him.

"You don't think—I mean, we can't be in any danger…"

"You know the old saying, *habiba*. Better safe than sorry."

She couldn't imagine what could happen to them on this luxurious dream of an island but she'd put her trust in Salim since the crash. It made no sense to doubt him now.

"Salim." She hesitated. "Are you really a sheikh? A prince?"

His lips twisted. "Yes. And don't remind me of how I must have sounded, making that ridiculous pronouncement."

Grace smiled. "It didn't sound ridiculous at

all. Jack went from looking as if he wanted to throw us into a dungeon to the most cordial host in the world."

Salim grinned as he walked slowly through the bedroom, opening built-in cupboards and peering into them, poking his head into the twin dressing rooms and the marble bathroom.

"Yes. That was the general idea. Titles can be a pain in the—uh, an anomaly in the twenty-first century but they still have some value in convincing people you're on the up-and-up." He looked down at his torn, sweat and grass stained clothes, then at Grace. "I had the feeling we needed to do something to convince him we were legitimate castaways, not a pair of burglars."

The idea of burglars, out here in the middle of nowhere, made Grace laugh. He'd hoped it would. She'd been through so much in, what, forty-eight hours? She looked better than she had a right to after they'd washed ashore. She looked beautiful, in fact, and his throat seemed to tighten at the realization. Still, she had color in her cheeks that he suspected might be more from fever than from the sun, the bruise on her temple was the deepest black and blue he'd ever seen, and it worried him that she still hadn't recovered her memory.

Most of all, he couldn't stop thinking about what had happened beside the waterfall.

She'd been wild with passion, completely uninhibited in his arms. She'd been the old Grace, not the one who'd made love with him the last couple of weeks before she'd run away when her lovemaking had grown reserved, when she'd seemed to observe the act more than experience it.

He'd noticed, but he hadn't said anything. What did it matter? Their affair had been going on too long, he'd told himself; maybe it was time to think about moving on.

But a little while ago—a little while ago, every kiss, every sigh, had told him she felt the way he did, as if they were drowning in pleasure.

Until those weeks before she'd left him, that was always how it had been with Grace. She'd never held anything back in bed.

Salim had known a lot of women—it was the natural result of being rich and powerful and what the gossip magazines called "a gorgeous stud." You were born with your looks—you didn't ask for them—and by the time he was eighteen, the young prince of a kingdom no longer torn by warring factions, but one guided by his father's steady hand and rich in newly discovered oil, he'd known he was a man who could have his pick of women.

They had flocked to him.

At that tender age, it was perfection.

In his freshman year at Harvard, he made fast friends with two other guys from his part of the world, both sheikhs, both princes, and when a sorority newsletter called the three of them "studly and gorgeous," they'd had a tough time pretending to feel offended.

Eventually, though, that combination of looks, money and power made them all long for anonymity.

Salim hated the way people fawned over him. He felt like a commodity, not a man; he learned to duck the media, to be almost paranoid about keeping his personal life private. He had all the most beautiful women a man could want but he never really knew if they wanted him, the man called Salim, or the Salim who was a prince.

After a while, it didn't matter.

Women came into a man's life and left it. No

ripples in the water when they did. He preferred it that way. He could have sex as intense as a man could want without the attendant problem of Forever.

Forever was a word that didn't even apply to oil fields, much less relationships.

And then, Grace came along.

She hadn't seemed to care about his title. She was unmoved by his wealth. She was without pretension. Their second date, he took her to dinner at a new restaurant in Chelsea. The reviews it had garnered were wonderful. "Fabulous" was the word everyone used to describe it.

Grace took a forkful of her entrée, chewed, swallowed… and waited while he took a forkful of his.

Whatever they'd been served, it was awful.

"So," he'd said, deadpan, "what do you think?"

Grace had leaned forward. "I think we should go to my place and I'll scramble us some eggs."

They did. They walked there, despite the fact that it had begun raining. When he said he'd call his driver, she stopped him.

"Let's just walk," she'd said.

"Walk?" he'd replied, as if she'd spoken in classical Greek.

He could still recall her smile. "It's just a summer shower and my apartment is only half a dozen blocks away. I love to walk in the rain, Salim. Don't you?"

In fact, he did. Growing up in the desert had left its mark. Rain was still something joyful. But Grace was wearing a white silk dress so chic and simple it had to be incredibly expensive, and shoes that he figured were Jimmy Choos or Manolo Blahniks. Her hair was loose on her shoulders. It looked casual but he had paid enough salon bills for mistresses over the years—not that he ever did for Grace, who'd refused to let him support her in any way—he had paid enough of those bills to recognize a three hundred dollar hairstyle when he saw it.

"Oh, come on," she'd said, taking his hand, tugging him along the sidewalk, and they'd walked in the rain, even done a little dance in a puddle at the corner of Spring and Broadway.

And instead of having scrambled eggs, they'd made love with a passion beyond anything he had ever known.

After, holding her in his arms in her demure double bed, her head on his shoulder, her hand over his heart, he'd wondered if it were possible, even remotely possible, that this woman was real, was honest, was as genuine as she seemed; that she wanted him, only him, not Sheikh Salim or Prince Salim…

Hell, no.

She'd wanted his money, he thought, and he came back to the present and the truth with ice in his heart. She had amnesia. So what? Suddenly staying here in this romantic hideaway seemed like a bad joke.

"Salim?"

He blinked and focused his gaze on Grace. She offered a tentative smile.

"You seem a million miles away."

A muscle knotted in his jaw. "Not quite that far," he said coolly. "Just a few thousand."

Her eyebrows rose. He explained.

"I was thinking about New York. My office. My life. And hoping it wasn't going to take much longer to return to it."

Grace's smile faded. "Oh." Her voice was low. "Oh, of course. This must be awful for you. Stuck in the middle of nowhere like this."

Had she hoped he'd say something romantic?

That he didn't want to go back to the world too soon? He couldn't blame her; a woman might see things that way, especially since they'd been a heartbeat away from having sex. But they hadn't, and he'd come to his senses. For a dangerous interval, he'd forgotten that this was not the real Grace. Under the sweetness, the passion, the real Grace still existed, the Grace who had played him for a fool, stolen his trust, his money, his—his—

Salim swung away, drove his hands deep into his trouser pockets and stared out toward the ocean.

"I'm sure you want a shower," he said gruffly. "Go ahead. I'll look around for Jack." He paused, then delivered what he knew would finish what they had almost begun. "I'm going to tell him that I'm taking a separate room."

Could a man actually hear silence?

He could hear it now.

"But you said…" Grace cleared her throat. "You said, until we were sure of things, we should—we should stay together."

He turned toward her. "I'm sure of things now, Grace."

She flinched as if he'd struck her. She wasn't stupid; he knew she'd gotten the message. He didn't want her. End of romantic island dalliance. For a minute, he told himself what a bastard he was. He'd have made love to her; another minute he'd have been deep inside her. Now he was rejecting her and because of her amnesia, she didn't have a clue as to the reason.

"That's excellent news." Her smile glittered but her eyes were bright with unshed tears. "I didn't want to push. I mean, I'm grateful for all you've done, but I'd really love some privacy."

She turned on her heel and walked into the adjoining master bath, head high, spine straight. The door swung shut.

Salim's jaw knotted. She was one hell of a woman, this Grace. Proud. Smart. Self-contained.

Too bad he knew what lay beneath the surface. Too bad he could envision what she was doing right now, behind that closed bathroom door. Unbuttoning his shirt. Slipping it from her shoulders. Unhooking her bra, letting it fall away from her breasts. Hooking her fingers into her panties, skimming them down her legs—her long, lovely legs—and stepping out of them, then standing in the shower, head back, eyes closed, letting the water caress her silken skin as the waterfall would have caressed it…

Except, he'd have been under that waterfall, too, standing in back of her, his arms around her. It would have been his hands that caressed her breasts, stroked her thighs, and she would have turned to him, lifted her face for his kisses, whispered that she wanted him, wanted him…

Anger at Grace, at himself, at the slyness of fate for dropping them onto this island together swept through him.

"Damn it," he said, and then he said the word louder and before he could think, before he could ask himself what in hell he was doing, Salim strode to the bathroom door, jiggled the knob, then snarled an oath, put his shoulder to the door and it flew open.

Grace stood at the vanity, still wearing his shirt, tears sliding like tiny diamonds down her face and his anger disappeared; something took its place that he didn't, couldn't identify.

"*Habiba,*" he said, "sweetheart, please, forgive me."

A sob broke from her throat and then she was in his arms, her face against his chest, her heart racing against his heart. He gathered her so tightly against him that there was no place at which his body ended and hers began and when she raised her face to his, when he looked deep into her tear-blurred eyes, he knew he was lost.

"Grace," he whispered, and her answering whispers, her soft "yes, yes, yes," fell like a sweet flame against his lips as he kissed her.

He wanted to do this slowly.

He had not made love to her in an eternity, had not held her, kissed her, felt her breasts against his chest, tasted the honey of her mouth.

But she was filled with the same fever that drove him. Her hands were hot against his skin. Her mouth drank from his. Her hips moved against his in invitation to a dance as old as time.

"Please," she said, and he reached for the buttons on her shirt, growled in frustration when his fingers seemed too big and clumsy to undo them, and solved the problem by tearing the shirt in half.

He tore away her bra, too; he was blind with hunger, with desire, with the compelling need to enter her, bind himself to her, and when her breasts tumbled into his waiting hands he bent to them, sucked the nipples, tongued them, bit lightly at her tender flesh and she cried out as she always had when he made love to her, and he knew she was racing with him to the edge.

He hooked his thumbs in her panties, knelt and pulled them down to her ankles. She put a hand on his shoulder and stepped free of them, raising first one foot and then the other, and he took merciless advantage of her posture, lifting his face to the swirl of soft curls between her thighs, seeking the bud that he'd always loved, tonguing it as Grace cried out his name.

He put his hand there, groaned as he felt her honeyed heat drench his palm.

"Grace," he said thickly, "my Grace…"

She bent to him, cupped his face, kissed his mouth and tasted the proof of her passion on his lips. He rose before her, still kissing her, and lifted her onto the vanity.

Their eyes met, his hot with desire, hers blurred with need. He tore off his trousers, his boxers, put his hands on her thighs and parted them. Eased forward so the head of his passion-swollen penis brushed her labia.

She moaned. Wondered if she might die of pleasure.

"Watch," he whispered, and she looked down at his erection as he slowly entered her and God oh God, he was so big, so beautiful, she knew it would be like this, that he would touch her like this, enter her like this. Knew that when she reached for him before he'd completely filled her, encircled him as much as her hand could manage, his breath would catch and he would say *Habiba, be careful, I'm close, so close...*

And she knew that when she took her hand away, he would thrust forward and fill her womb, her heart, her soul.

Salim's hands gripped her hips. Slowly, slowly enough to kill her with the pleasure of it, he filled her. Grace trembled; she saw only him, only Salim, his beautiful body glittering with sweat as he took her closer and closer to the edge of the universe. Her fingers dug into his shoulders as he drew back, then eased into her again.

"Not yet," he said through his teeth. "Not yet..."

"Yes," she commanded, "yes. Now, Salim, now..."

And he was lost.

He drove deep, hard; her womb convulsed around him as she screamed his name and in the last seconds before he emptied himself into her, he looked into her eyes and thought, *She is mine. Forever and ever, mine, mine…*

He groaned Grace's name. She dug her hands into his hair, kissed his mouth, sobbed with joy at his possession and Salim let go and flew with her into the paradise that had always belonged only to them.

Seconds slipped by, became minutes.

Grace sat slumped on the marble vanity, her arms looped around Salim's neck, her face pressed against his shoulder. He had fallen forward against her, his face against her breasts.

His arms still held her fast.

After a long time, he sighed.

"I think we'd better move, *habiba,*" he said in a husky whisper.

"Mmm."

Her voice, soft and sated, made him smile.

"Was that a 'yes'?"

"Mmm."

He gave a low chuckle and pressed a kiss to her breast.

"I'm going to put you on your feet, *habiba*. Okay?"

She nodded. Her hair was a whisper of silk across his face. God, how he had missed her. Missed this, making love to her, holding her afterward, feeling their heartbeats slow in unison.

"On the count of three, then…"

"How about on the count of one million?" she whispered, and gave a low, husky laugh. It was the sexiest laugh in the world; he'd never forgotten the delicious shock of hearing it and realizing it was a part of the elegant, supremely business-like Grace Hudson no one but he knew existed.

Salim grinned, lifted her from the counter, let her slide down his body until her feet touched the marble floor. He framed her face with his hands, tilted it to his and gave her a long, deep kiss.

"Are you all right?" he said softly.

"Oh, yes," she answered, her kiss-swollen lips curving in a smile. "I am very all right. That was—it was—"

"Wonderful. Perfect."

Another smile. "Yes."

He leaned his forehead against hers. "As your doctor—"

"My doctor?"

"Certainly. Didn't I treat your bruises? Didn't I remove a thorn from your foot?"

She laughed softly. "As my doctor, what?"

"Well, I'm going to tell you what you need."

"Which is?"

"A shower. A meal. A glass of champagne." He gave her a slow, deep kiss. "And more of what we just did, *habiba*. Lots and lots more, but in that big bed in the other room, on those silk sheets. How does that sound?"

"It sounds just right," Grace said, and lifted her mouth for another kiss.

He swept her into his arms, carried inside the huge glass-walled shower, filled his hands with lather and washed her carefully from head to toe. She did the same for him. And, somehow, their hands slowed.

Her breasts, her thighs, the sweet tawny curls that guarded the heart of her femininity seemed to require extra attention from him.

His chest, his flat belly, seemed to require the same thing from her, and Grace's strokes grew slower as Salim's length grew longer until he was hard and erect and magnificent in her hands.

She dropped to her knees, caressed him, cupped him, then drew him into her mouth.

His hands fastened in her hair.

"Grace," he said in warning, his voice hoarsening. "Grace…"

He looked down, watched her minister to him, and the power of what he felt for her tore through him.

"Grace," he whispered, and he drew her to her feet, sought her mouth, lifted her in his arms and braced his shoulders against the wall as he entered her, filled her, emptied himself deep inside her while her soft cries and the steam of the water mingled.

Gently he lowered her to her feet. Let the water sluice down on them both. Then he stepped from the shower, wrapped her in a towel, carried her to the bed and lay down without letting go of her. Moonlight streamed through the French doors.

"Look," Grace whispered. "A shooting star!"

Salim followed her gaze, just in time to see a brilliant light fall across the night sky and into the ocean. He gathered her close against him. Another star blazed against the darkness, and another and another and another.

Grace turned in his arms.

"Such a beautiful gift to give me, Salim," she said, smiling. "A sky alive with shooting stars. I'll never see one again without remembering this wonderful night."

He was the one who had been given a gift, he thought, as he kissed her. This perfect island. This paradise, and another chance to be with the Grace he had once known…

But it wouldn't last.

They would be found. The world would intrude. The truth of why they were here, together, would come between them.

No, he thought fiercely. He couldn't let that happen.

His last thought, before he followed Grace into sleep, was that he could not imagine letting go of her ever again.

When they woke, they dressed in clothes they took from the built-in cupboards.

Faded denims and a white T-shirt for him. Pale yellow shorts and a dark blue tank top for her. She found a scrunchie in a drawer of the vanity, brushed her hair back from her face and secured it in a ponytail. Then she peered into the mirror and wrinkled her nose.

"You'd think there'd at least be a lipstick and some mascara in a fairyland like this," she grumbled.

Salim came up behind her, wrapped his arms around her and smiled at her in the mirror.

"Stop fishing for compliments, woman. You know you look beautiful just the way you are."

She smiled. "So do you."

"Me?" His smile became a grin. "I haven't shaved in, what, three days? My nose is as red as a boiled lobster claw." He spun her toward him. "Besides, what self-respecting male would ever think of himself as 'beautiful?'"

"Ah. My mistake." Her arms looped around his neck. "Okay, you're not beautiful. You're spectacular. How's that?"

"Much better," he said solemnly, and kissed her.

The kiss deepened. Grace put her hands on Salim's chest and gave him a gentle shove.

"Food," she said. "And lots of it, before anything else."

He grinned. "You're right. We'll need our energy for what I have planned for tonight."

"And those plans are…?"

He told her, in vivid detail, and she blushed so becomingly that he just had to kiss her again, and despite all her talk about needing energy, they tumbled back into bed and made slow, tender love.

Afterward, Grace stretched like a cat.

"If you don't feed me soon," she warned, "I'm liable to fade away like the heroine in a Victorian novel."

Salim jumped to his feet, held out his hand, drew her up beside him and slapped her lightly on the backside.

"I'll give you two minutes to get your clothes on. After that, I'm going to go to the dining room by myself and by the time you get there, I'll have eaten everything but the plates."

The dining room sideboard was laden with chilled dishes of shrimp, lobster, salads and fruit. There was an urn of coffee, crystal pitchers of fresh orange juice and iced mint tea.

They ate. And, as Grace said, laughing, they ate some more.

When they'd finished, they walked out the open doors—all the doors in the house stood open to the incredible beauty that surrounded it—and stood watching the sun go down, Salim with his arm around Grace's waist, she with her head on his shoulder.

"Salim," she said softly, "I'm very happy."

He kissed her forehead as he turned her to him. "So am I, *habiba*."

"But—but it seems strange to be so happy."

He held his breath. What did she remember?

"I mean—I mean, it's as if there's something, some reason I'm not supposed to feel like this." She tilted her face up to his. "Something besides the fact that I have amnesia. Does that sound crazy?"

Did it? Not when you realized he was the one who shouldn't feel happy. The woman in his arms had stolen from him—but she hadn't. The woman in his arms wasn't the woman who'd done the stealing, and if thinking like *that* wasn't crazy, what was?

"Salim?"

"No," he said slowly, "it doesn't sound crazy at all. You've gone through a lot, *habiba*. Why would anyone be surprised if your thoughts are a little confused?"

She nodded, though he could see she wasn't convinced.

"I just wish…" Her voice shook and she cleared her throat. "I just wish I could remember things. Anything," she said, with a sad little laugh. "Anything at all."

He drew her close against him. She sighed and leaned her head against his shoulder as he ran his hand up and down her spine.

"You will," he promised. "I'm sure you will. Which reminds me—how does your head feel?"

"It's fine."

"No pain?"

"None." She smiled. "It certainly does look, um, interesting, though. Did you ever see such colors?"

Salim grinned, lifted her face to his and kissed her. "The blue is most becoming."

"Thank you, kind sir. You've made me feel much better."

"Have I?" His eyes darkened; he drew her to her toes and kissed her until she moaned and clung to his shoulders. "I can make you feel better yet," he said softly, and when she smiled, he lifted her into his arms and carried her to their bedroom.

* * *

In the middle of the night, Salim suddenly awoke and knew he was alone.

"Grace?"

He sat up. The room was bathed in moonlight and Grace was standing in the open doorway that led to the terrace, a length of pale, flowered silk tied around her like a sarong, her hair streaming in glorious disarray down her back.

"*Habiba,*" he said, as he swung his legs to the floor.

She didn't stir. Salim pulled on his shorts but left them unzipped as he went to her and placed his hands lightly on her shoulders. He drew her back against him, bent his head and kissed the curve of her neck and shoulder. Her body was stiff, almost rigid. Had her memory returned? Not yet, he prayed, by Ishtar, not yet. His mind was crowded with questions; he had to work through them before he was ready to deal with reality.

"Grace," he said softly. "What's wrong, sweetheart?"

She swallowed. Then, slowly, she turned in his arms, looked up into his eyes.

"Salim. I—I remember."

His pulse quickened. "What do you remember, *habiba?*"

"Not who I am. Not my life. I just—I remember you."

She hesitated and he cleared his throat. "You remember me?"

"Yes. No. That's not right. I don't remember you. Not *you,* Salim. What I remember is—is the feel of you against me. The taste of you. I remember that I never wanted to be anywhere but with you, in your arms, but—but I can't remember anything else. Not how we met or where, or what our lives were like, or what we were to each other. All I know is that when you touch me, the world is right and perfect and—and—" She began to weep. "And—and I know, I *know* that just when I thought I had everything I could possibly want, that I had you, something terrible happened and I lost you, I lost you…"

She fell against him, her body racked with sobs.

Salim cursed softly and swept her into his arms. He carried her to the bed and sat down with her in his lap, cradling her, rocking her until her weeping stopped.

"It's going to be all right," he crooned. "I promise, *habiba*."

He gathered her against him, pressed kisses into her hair and knew it was time he faced two incontrovertible facts.

The first was that despite all the proof he'd seen, he knew that his Grace had never embezzled or stolen anything in her life.

The second was that he loved her.

CHAPTER TEN

GRACE wound her arms around Salim's neck and pressed her cheek against his chest.

He was solid and safe. He was her rock.

How, *how* could she have forgotten everything about her life? As much as she tried not to think about it, the realization was always there. She felt the way a child would feel, believing there was a monster in the closet. You could ignore it, you could think about a dozen other things, but in the back of your mind you knew the monster was there, just waiting to pop out.

The only place she felt secure was in Salim's arms. His strength and his tenderness were her safe harbor. Now, as he whispered words of comfort, gently stroked his hand down her back, touched his lips lightly to her hair, the soul-swallowing emptiness that came of not remembering faded away.

Without him… She shuddered and burrowed closer. She didn't want to think about what enduring this nightmare would be like without her lover.

Her lover?

Yes. The words felt so right. This man, this stranger, was her lover. Now and in the past. She couldn't recall her own name, but her heart and body knew his and though the knowing had nothing to do with logic, it was real. It had to do with this, the way he held her. This, the way he touched her. This, the way even his scent gave her solace.

"Easy, sweetheart," he said softly, rocking her in his embrace.

His lips left a trail of tender kisses over her hair, her bruised temple, her cheek. She lifted her face to his; he kissed her mouth and she sighed at the gentleness of it.

He asked nothing, gave everything and, gradually, she wanted, needed more.

Her lips clung to his. Parted under his. Her hand cupped his nape; his hands threaded into her hair and she moved even closer to him, hot skin against hot skin.

How she loved this. Loved being held by him. Loved making love with him. Loved—oh God, loved him. He was not a stranger. He was part of the life she was struggling so hard to remember.

But if they'd been lovers, why wouldn't he talk about it? Why wouldn't he tell her what it was they had been to each other?

Grace drew back. "Salim." His thick, dark lashes lifted; his eyes were blurred with desire. "Salim. Please, you have to tell me everything. I need to know about you. About us—"

"Later," he said, his voice deep and dark and deliciously sexy, and he bent her back over his arm, drew one of her nipples deep into his mouth, and she sank into a whirlpool of pleasure.

Someone slipped a note under their door. Breakfast would be served on the terrace overlooking the garden whenever they wished.

They showered, chose shorts and shirts from the dressing rooms. Racks held endless pairs of sandals that were obviously brand-new, but bare feet seemed a better choice for the casual elegance that surrounded them.

The big teak terrace seemed to meld into the

garden, which was in full, glorious bloom. A table shaded by a white umbrella took center stage; nearby, an elaborate buffet was laid out on trays spread across a long glass table. Grace's eyes widened. There were pitchers of fresh juice, bowls of fruit, a platter of shrimp in coconut sauce, another of cold lobster, a chafing dish that held eggs and bacon…

Salim served her, heaping her plate high.

"I couldn't possibly eat all that," she protested—and then, to his unabashed delight, she turned her own words inside out. When finally she gave a mock groan, put her hands on her belly and said she'd never eaten that much in her life, he grinned, wrapped his hand around the back of her neck and tugged her toward him.

"Thank you for the compliment, *habiba*." She raised her eyebrows and he laughed softly. "Great sex does wonders for the appetite."

She laughed and said he was right, but her heart told her it was more than sex. Much, much more.

A smiling girl in a sarong bought fragrant coffee and a basket of tiny, still-warm pastries. Once she'd left, Grace leaned toward the basket, her lovely face rapt with concentration, the tip of her tongue peeping out from between her lips.

Salim thought of how many times he'd seen her do the same thing when they'd had dinner at Per Se or Aureole, agonizing over the damage that could be done by sinfully dark chocolate and heavy cream.

More proof, as if he needed it, that this was the same Grace she'd always been. The Grace he'd fallen in love with, even if he had been too stubborn to admit it to himself.

He chose a pastry and brought it to her lips.

"So many calories," she murmured, with longing in her eyes.

Was that longing for the éclair...or for him?

"Take a taste, *habiba,*" he said softly. "Part your lips for me."

Color flooded her cheeks. "Salim…"

He leaned closer. "Open," he whispered.

She did; she bit lightly into the tiny pastry, licked her upper lip at the sudden explosion of chocolate and whipped cream.

"Delicious," she said, and watched her lover's eyes grow dark.

"Let me see," he said, and covered her mouth

with his, sharing the rich tastes of chocolate and cream and Grace, Grace above all because the taste of her was more wonderful than anything the culinary gods could possibly invent.

He kissed her again and again, and when she trembled in his arms, when he could feel the need building inside him, he drew her from the table to a chaise longue and slid his hand between her thighs.

Grace caught her breath. "Someone might see us," she whispered, even as she arched toward him.

"Look at me, *habiba*," Salim said thickly, "at me and nothing else."

Then he slipped his hand higher, found her, found her wet and warm, and Grace forgot everything but her lover and the magic of their passion.

After, she dozed in his arms.

Salim held her close, watched her as she slept, so sweetly trusting in his embrace. Guilt twisted his gut. If she knew why she was marooned on this island with him, that he had believed her a thief, that he'd all but forced her on the plane with him, she would not be lying with him like this.

It would all come out, when they were found. He

had to find a way to tell her the truth before then but, heaven help him, he didn't know how to do it.

She sighed and turned her face against his shoulder.

He dropped a soft kiss on her hair.

How many times had she slept in his arms? How often had he felt the welcome weight of her head on his shoulder, the whisper of her breath on his throat? How often had he held her close and been consumed by a fiery rush of pure masculine pride that Grace, this woman of beauty, strength and intellect, was his mistress?

And wasn't that one hell of a way to describe their relationship? Not just because Grace had never permitted him to support her financially but because the word was a lie.

Months ago, before his world had come undone, he'd sat in a quiet bar in lower Manhattan with the two friends who knew him better than anyone else. Tariq and Khalil, both newly wed, had talked about their wives; they'd joked and rolled their eyes and said, man, it was tough, being married.

He'd missed or maybe simply ignored the happiness in their smiles and he'd said, with all the arrogance of bachelorhood, well, he wasn't surprised to hear it, and that was one of the reasons he was happy with the status quo.

"Aha," Tariq had said, winking at Khalil, "our boy has himself a new lover."

"A mistress," he'd replied, "not a lover. There's an enormous difference between the two."

His pals had grinned. "And that difference is?" Khalil had said.

"The L word," Tariq had replied before Salim could answer. "L-O-V-E. The sheikh of Senahdar doesn't believe in it."

To this moment, he could remember the change that had come over his pals' faces.

"Someday, he will," Khalil had said softly.

"If he's lucky," Tariq had added.

And Salim had laughed and bought the next round of drinks to show them how wrong they were.

"To mistresses," he'd said, raising his glass of Johnny Walker Blue. "Or, in the words of that old Tina Turner song, 'What's love got to do with it?'"

Everything, he thought now. It was what he felt for Grace, what had made him come after her, what had almost killed him when he'd learned about her supposed theft because his heart had wanted to believe she loved him long before his brain had caught up to the truth.

Grace stirred. Her lashes lifted; she looked at him and gave him a lazy smile.

"Was I asleep?" she said softly.

He bent his head and kissed her, taking his time with the kiss, sinking into the softness of her lips and sipping from their honeyed sweetness.

"No, *habiba*. I am the one who was asleep." He drew a breath. "But I am wide-awake at last," he said, drawing her up with him. "Why don't we take a walk?"

Hand in hand, they went walking slowly along the beach.

The white sand seemed to stretch forever; the incredibly blue water of the curving horizon glittered like sapphires under the midday sun.

Grace exclaimed over pale pink and cream seashells. They paused to watch half a dozen small white birds poke for their lunch in the wet sand whenever a wave receded from the shore. It was the kind of lazy afternoon that could have stretched on for hours and hours, but Salim knew he was running out of the luxury of time.

How to begin? With what? Perhaps it was best to let Grace set the pace, he decided, and cleared his throat.

"*Habiba.* I know you have some questions you want answered."

Grace sighed. "Some? Only about a thousand."

"And I've put off answering them."

She turned to him, her expression suddenly grave. "Are you saying you'll answer them now?"

He nodded. "As best I can."

He'd expected her to show excitement, even begin peppering him with questions. To his surprise, she said nothing. Instead she stopped walking, stepped in front of him, put her hands on his chest and looked into his eyes.

"What if—what if this isn't a good idea?"

He almost laughed. Wasn't that supposed to be his line?

"I know I've been driving you crazy, pleading for you to tell me things but—but…"

He cupped her face. "But?"

"But…" She shook her head. "I don't know.

What if the things you tell me aren't things I want to hear?"

She sensed something. Well, why wouldn't she? He'd been evasive. That, alone, would have been a warning.

"Some of them will be," he said softly. "I have made mistakes, *habiba*. Terrible mistakes. I ask that you remember that I am only a man and that men are fallible."

That made her smile. "Why do I get the feeling that's a rare admission, coming from you?"

He smiled, too, took her hand and they started walking again. He told himself to stop being such a damned coward but he didn't know where to begin.

For that matter, he didn't know where to end, either.

Much of what he had to tell her was sweet but the part that covered the last few months was bitter. She'd just told him she was fearful of what he would say. How much, then, was she ready to hear? Were you supposed to tell someone with amnesia everything she had forgotten? Could it be harmful, especially when those forgotten things included a felony she was supposed to have committed? A felony he was now certain she had not committed, despite the evidence against her?

But he had believed it. He would have to admit that. And he'd have to tell her the rest, that he'd gone after her to bring her back to face the law.

He didn't want to think about her reaction to hearing that.

God! There had to be a way to do this so it made sense. He tried to gather his thoughts into something cohesive but the more he tried, the more impossible it became.

Just begin at the beginning, he told himself, but where was that? Was it when she came to work for him? When they started spending time together at the office? Was it that first time they'd made love or the time they'd danced in the rain, or the time she'd watched him change that flat while they both froze their tails off?

Or was it the time they'd quarreled over something foolish and she'd slammed down the phone and he'd gone straight to her apartment and when she opened the door, he'd stepped inside, kicked the door shut behind him and made love to her right there, against the foyer wall, and when she was still trembling with the aftermath of their passion, he'd told her that she would never do that to him again and she said she would do whatever she pleased to anyone she pleased, that he didn't own her, he couldn't tell her what to do, and he'd said she'd better get used to the idea that she belonged to him, only to him…

And she had.

The trouble was, he'd never admitted that he belonged to her.

Was it that growing awareness that had made him start to draw away from her? He'd known it; he'd told himself it was just the natural course of things but then he'd begun planning that damned trip to California and he'd suddenly realized that he didn't want to go there or anywhere without Grace.

He'd decided to surprise her. He told no one of his change in plans. Well, no one except his new CFO, Thomas Shipley, who'd have to do without Grace for the week.

"I need Ms. Hudson's expertise for this series of meetings," he'd said, and Shipley had smiled in a knowing way and said of course, Ms. Hudson had surely made herself indispensable.

What, Salim had thought, did that mean? Not just what Shipley had said but the way he'd said it, and the little smile that had accompanied the words.

And then he'd thought about other things.

About how he'd broken his own rules, getting involved with an employee. About how exciting it had been to deal with a woman who'd met him on his own terms, no games or nonsense, just an admission that she wanted him as a man, not as a sheikh or a prince.

About what Shipley had said. *Ms. Hudson had surely made herself indispensable.*

He changed his plans.

Flew to the coast without her. Phoned her only twice that entire week, not a dozen times a day the way he really wanted. And when he called her the last time and she said she could hardly wait to see him, that she'd booked them into an isolated cabin on a lake in the Adirondack Mountains so they could spend the weekend alone he'd said—God, he could hardly bear to remember it—he'd said he'd be much too busy for a weekend in the Adirondacks and he'd hung up.

He flew home the day after that.

And Grace was gone. Grace, and the money,

and when he had to suffer the humiliation of calling Shipley to try to figure out what had happened, there was the further humiliation of Shipley telling him that he'd been developing doubts about Ms. Hudson for several months now and he'd been afraid to say anything because, well, everyone knew the change in Ms. Hudson's relationship with the sheikh and now he wished he'd spoken up because ten million was a hell of a lot of money…

Ten million was a hell of a lot of money.

Shipley had said it; he could still hear him saying it. The thing was, Shipley had said it before Salim had even mentioned the amount that was missing.

He looked at Grace, walking beside him. He wanted to drop to his knees, beg her forgiveness, tell her everything that had happened was his fault, that he'd let pride and ego and fear, damn it, fear of his feelings for her destroy the best thing that had ever happened to him.

Grace's small hand tightened on his. "Salim," she said, into the growing silence, "is whatever you're going to tell me that awful?"

He cleared his throat. "What I have to tell you is—it's complicated, *habiba.*"

"Then, how about starting with something simple?"

None of this was simple but he was willing to try. "For instance?"

She smiled at him. "Well, tell me what a sheikh does."

He blinked. It wasn't the question he had expected. "What does he do?"

"What do *you* do? You won't tell me about me, then tell me about you. What's a sheikh's life like?" She smiled again. "Do you ride the desert on a magnificent white stallion? Do you steal women and make wild love to them in your tent?"

He smiled, brought her hand to his lips and kissed her knuckles.

"Such stereotypes, *habiba*. I think you must be a fan of very old movies."

"Seriously, what does a sheikh do?"

"I only know what I do."

"And what's that?"

She was still smiling but he could tell that she was serious. That was how his Grace had always been, eager to discover things, to learn the intricacies of his bank, to learn about him—not that he'd told her much about himself. That was another of his relationship rules. He didn't talk about himself, the real Salim al Taj. Why tell anyone what it had been like to be a boy caught in a nightmare?

"I own a private investment firm."

Grace's eyebrows rose. "Private, as in all yours?"

"Private, as in part of it belongs to me and my family and part belongs to my people."

"Your people. Yes. I almost forgot. You said you were a prince."

"I am." He smiled. "And no, I don't sit on a throne and wear a crown."

"What do you do, then?"

His smile tilted. "I prepare for the day when I will lead my nation."

She danced out in front of him and put her hands on his shoulders, bringing them both to a halt.

"Serious stuff," she said softly.

Salim nodded. "Yes."

"Was your childhood serious, too? Tutors? Boarding schools? No time to play or be a little boy?"

He wanted to sweep her into his arms. No one, in his entire life, had ever wondered about the effects of his childhood, not even his father who loved him deeply, but who saw him as a vessel to be filled with responsibility for Senahdar.

"It was very serious," he said, and before he knew it, he was telling her all of it.

The ugly philosophical battle between those who wanted to remain in the past and those who wanted to step into the future that had, inevitably, became an actual war. The escape to the desert, the harsh realities of life there, the deaths of his uncle and cousins before those loyal to his father had finally resumed control. He spoke of his loneliness. The fear, the sorrow of a child thrust too soon into the realities of the world and then the eye-opening moment he'd arrived at Harvard and realized he was a stranger in a strange land. He talked about the two young sheikhs who had befriended him, how they had become the brothers he'd always longed to have. How he had formulated a plan to take the funds now pouring in from Senahdar's oil fields and use them to make better lives for his people.

And then he fell silent, horrified at how all that had spilled from his lips, reluctant to look at Grace and see what he was sure would be reflected in her eyes.

He had stripped away the polished Western veneer of the man he'd become and shown her who he was underneath, and she would be appalled by it, by him—

"Oh, Salim," she whispered.

She rose on her toes, clasped his face, brought his mouth to hers and kissed him as no one ever had, with tenderness and compassion and complete acceptance of who he was.

"You're a wonderful man," she said. Tears glittered in her eyes. "No wonder I—no wonder I— I cared for you so deeply." She drew a shuddering breath. "I did, didn't I? I cared for you with all my heart?"

Salim cupped her shoulders and drew her to him. "We cared for each other, *habiba,*" he said huskily. "I was just too much a fool to admit it."

Grace nodded. She had suspected as much, that their relationship, whatever its complexity, had not been equally balanced.

"How did we meet?"

He took her hand and led her toward the house. They had been walking for a very long time. Late afternoon shadows were slipping across the land; the sun was beginning its descent into the sea.

"You came to work for me."

"As what?"

He brought her hand to his lips and kissed her fingertips. "You were assistant to my CFO. My chief fin—"

"Chief financial officer." She frowned. "I don't know how I know that title, but I do. Go on. How did we—get involved?"

"We didn't get involved," he said gruffly. "We became lovers. I think I'd wanted you from the minute I saw you." He smiled. "And I think it was the same for you."

Grace laughed softly. "Rudolph Valentino couldn't have said it better." She blinked. "Rudolph Valentino? The movies you teased me about before... He was an actor in one of them, wasn't he? A silent screen classic?" Her face lit. "Do you think I'm getting my memory back? I mean—I'm starting to recall other things. Things from long ago. Like that Girl Scout memory. And—and working at a place where I grilled hamburgers—"

"You grilled hamburgers?"

She looked up at him, laughing at the startled expression on his face. "I think so. Didn't you know that about me?"

Salim shook his head. "No, *habiba*," he said softly. "We didn't—we never really talked much about our lives."

"We didn't?"

He shook his head again. "But we will, Grace. I promise. Once your memory returns, we'll share everything."

She gave a long sigh. "I hope it returns soon."

He hoped so, too—but he was selfish enough to want to tell her everything before it did, that he knew he'd been wrong about her, that she could never have been anything but the incredible woman he'd known her to be.

That he loved her.

"I think it will," he said gently. "But don't push it, *habiba*. Give it time to return slowly."

"Yes. I will. It's just that I want to remember so badly…" She hesitated. "Where were we going, when the plane crashed?"

"We were going to New York. From Bali."

"Bali. That's a long, long way from New York. Were we on vacation or was it a business trip?"

"It was—it was a business trip, *habiba*. Look, I don't think we should push this any further. I mean, we've covered a lot of ground today and—

and maybe we should let the rest come to you in its own time."

"You don't want to tell me the rest," she said, her eyes searching his.

"No," he said quickly, "no, sweetheart, I do. I just—I just—" He cursed himself for his cowardice, gathered her to him and kissed her. "My life was empty until you entered it," he said, and took a shaky breath. He owed her the truth but what did he tell her first, that he loved her…or that he'd believed her capable of the worst kind of duplicity?

"What happened after I came to work for you? Did we start to date right away?"

"We avoided anything more than 'hello, goodbye, yes, no, please, and thank you' at first." He smiled. "We were both very proper. But we had to spend some evenings working late and, one of those evenings, I surprised myself by asking if you wanted to see me Sunday afternoon."

Grace smiled. "And I, of course, said 'yes.'"

Salim grinned. "Well, certainly, *habiba*. I am a sheikh, after all." She laughed. He kissed her and they walked on. "I took you to a gallery in Soho." He grinned. "I wanted to impress you with my cultural expertise."

She tilted her head up to him. "And did you?"

"I said the artist was amazing. You said he was incredible. Hours later, I admitted I thought the guy was amazingly awful, and you admitted you thought he was incredibly untalented."

That won him a delighted peal of laughter. He thought how he loved the way she laughed, the way she felt in the curve of his arm, the way the wind ruffled her hair.

"What made us decide to be honest?"

Salim stopped and turned her to him. He framed her face with his hands and gave her a long, slow, deep kiss.

"We made love," he said in a husky whisper.

She grinned. "On our first date?"

"And every possible moment after that. We made love everywhere, *habiba*. In my penthouse. In your apartment." Another long, slow, deep kiss. "In the back of my limo, in my office… We made love all the time, and still we could never get enough of each other."

"No," she whispered, "I don't think—I don't think I could ever have enough of you, Salim. Even now, after I spent the night, the morning, so many hours in your arms, I want you again. I want you kissing me, I want you holding me, I want you inside me…"

He took her mouth with his in a savage, soul-searing kiss. Grace wound her arms around his neck; he lifted her into his arms and carried her to a white canvas pavilion set under a pair of tall palms. The pavilion held a double sun chaise; he lay her on it and came down beside her.

"I love you," she said. "I know that I do—and I know that I shouldn't say it but I do, I do, I do—"

He silenced her with another kiss. Then he drew back just enough so he could look into her eyes.

"You can say it," he whispered. "I want you to say it, Grace. Because it is the only truth that matters. No matter what else I tell you, believe this. I am your love, as you are mine. I adore you, *habiba*. I will always adore you."

He undressed her with exquisite slowness, then stripped off his own clothes. Grace reached for him, wrapped her legs around his hips and Salim thrust deep into her body.

Into her soul.

Into her heart.

CHAPTER ELEVEN

GRACE lay back on the sugar-white sand, propped on her elbows as she watched her lover emerge from the sea.

The sun shone down on him; drops of water glittered like tiny jewels in his dark hair and on his tanned, hard body.

Her lips curved in a smile.

He was beautiful. So beautiful. Broad shoulders, muscled arms and chest, flat belly, narrow hips and long, tightly muscled legs…

Beautiful was the only way to describe him.

And he was hers.

He had told her he was, all through the day and then through another star-filled night, proved it to her with his words, his kisses, his caresses. Not that he had to prove it. She felt it, knew it, believed it with every inch of her being. This strong, tender, magnificent man belonged to her.

And she belonged to him.

A tremor went through her at the thought.

She still didn't know anything about herself beyond what Salim had told her, but instinct said she was not a woman who had ever wanted to "belong" to anyone. She knew, somehow, that she believed in female independence, in being an individual and not some man's possession—some man's toy—and yet, the realization that she was Salim's filled her with joy.

Belonging to him, loving him so much that you couldn't tell where you ended and he began, was somehow what she had waited for her entire life.

He smiled as he came toward her. Her heart lifted at the sight. He was everything to her—and yet, a hint of darkness shadowed her happiness. There was something he had not yet explained. She knew it as surely as she knew he was going to scoop up his towel, rub it over his hair and torso, then drop onto the quilted cotton beach blanket beside her…

Wrong.

Grace shrieked as he threw himself down next

to her dripping wet, grabbed her and rolled her beneath him.

"Hey," she said, trying to sound indignant, "do I look like a towel?"

His grin was purely, sexily male.

"I don't think so, *habiba,* but let me see…" He ran his hand over her as she squirmed in pretended protest, lightly cupping a breast, sliding it over her bare midriff, running it over her belly and then between her thighs. "Mmm. No, you don't feel the least bit like a towel to me."

"Well," she said, "I'm glad to hear it." Smiling, she wrapped her arms around his neck. "You're hot as the sun," she whispered. Her tongue darted out; she licked his shoulder. "And salty as the ocean. A very nice combination."

Salim returned the favor, lightly tasting her mouth, her throat, then nuzzling her bikini top away and running the tip of his tongue over her exposed nipple.

"Delicious," he said huskily.

Grace sighed and closed her eyes. Perfect, she thought lazily. All of it. Perfect. The place. The sun. The sea. And the man. Without question, the man. They were marooned on an island in the middle of the South Pacific with no way to contact the rest of the world, she couldn't remember anything that had ever happened to her before three days ago and yet, she was happy. So happy.

Too happy, a sly voice deep within her whispered.

It had whispered the same thing before, in the earliest hours of the morning when she'd awakened to the slow play of Salim's hands and mouth over her eager flesh but desire and the darkness had driven the unwanted whisper away. Now, in the bright light of day, the warning seemed more ominous, more determined…

Or, perhaps, more real.

"Why the frown, *habiba?*"

She looked up into the pale eyes of her lover. He was attuned to her every mood; she had never before been with a man so aware of her emotions. Not that she'd been with a lot of men. There'd been that Canadian lecturer in finance at grad school and then one of the associates at the first place she'd worked in New York, but that was hardly a lot of…

Her breath caught. Grad school. Her first job in finance. Two men and yes, she could recall their names and faces…

"Grace? What's the matter?"

"Nothing," she said with a little laugh. "Or maybe something. I don't know. I was—I was—my thoughts were wandering and then, all of a sudden, I remembered."

She could feel the sudden tension ripple through his body.

"Remembered what?"

"Nothing important. Two—two people I once knew. Graduate school. A place I worked…" She swallowed dryly. "Maybe—maybe my memory's coming back."

A muscle flickered in Salim's jaw. Maybe it was, and wouldn't it be a hell of a thing if she remembered all that he'd been avoiding telling her?

"Salim? Do you think it is?"

Stop being a coward, he told himself, and he sat up and drew her onto his lap.

"Yes, *habiba.* I think it probably is."

She nodded, touched his mouth with the tip of one finger, trailed it down his chin, down his neck and hard chest.

"So—so, is that good…or is it bad?"

There it was again, the hint that something— her mind, her psyche, perhaps just basic animal instinct—was warning that remembering was not going to be altogether joyful. Well, it wouldn't be, but which would be better? That she suddenly knew the real truth of their relationship, that they had not been together for months, that he had followed her to Bali, demanded she leave with him, refused to take her to San Francisco because he was determined to take her to New York and charge her with embezzlement?

Or that he wanted to hold her like this, forever. Kiss her like this. Look into her eyes, let her look into his while he explained that he loved her, that he'd always loved her even though he'd never admitted it to her or even to himself, that someone had set her up and he'd fallen for it, believed she was a liar, a thief, a cheat…

"Salim."

He forced his racing thoughts together. All that mattered was Grace, and not his selfish hope that she would understand. The one thing he could do for her now was tell her the absolute truth—and then pray that she loved him enough to forgive him.

"Yes," he said, and brushed a strand of hair from her eyes. "I heard what you asked me, sweetheart." He took a deep, deep breath. "It is good, that your memory is returning. It is also bad…not for you, but for me."

"I don't understand."

"No." He tried to smile but the stiffness of his lips told him he hadn't succeeded. "How could you, when these past days have been so perfect? But—but there are things you need to hear, Grace."

She nodded; the look of trepidation she gave him said she'd suspected as much all along. "Tell me," she whispered.

Salim cleared his throat. "What I told you about us is true, *habiba*. We were lovers. But—but our relationship floundered months ago." *Floundered?* He took another steadying breath. "You left me."

"I left you?" she said in bewilderment. "Why?"

He hesitated, then offered her the understatement of the year. "It's complicated, *habiba*."

"Did you go after me?"

"No." Her eyes went as wide as a frightened doe's. He lifted her face to his, somehow telling himself that if her eyes remained on his, if her skin bore his touch, she would understand that he had been a fool.

"Things ended between us. You went far away. I remained in New York. And we had nothing to do with each other after that until I learned you lived on the West Coast and that you worked for a private bank and that you were going to a conference in Bali…"

He was rushing his words together as if that could make the tale simpler and forestall the dawning awareness of the past on her face that terrified him.

"I lived in San Francisco," she said slowly, "but before that, I lived in Manhattan."

"Yes."

"My apartment was all the way downtown. But you lived on Fifth Avenue. Across from the park." Grace's brow furrowed. "We didn't live together." A statement, not a question. "I remember wishing we did but you never asked."

"No." God, this was agony. "I thought we were…" *Damn it, tell it straight!* "I thought I was too independent to share my life so completely with a woman."

"With me," she said in a hurt voice, and Salim cursed, drew her closer and kissed her.

"I was a fool, *habiba*. I loved you but I was too much a coward to admit it."

Her smile filled his heart. "I can't imagine you as a coward, Salim." Her smile faded. "But why did I leave you? Did I stop loving you?" She shook her head from side to side. "I couldn't have stopped loving you. I could never do that."

Salim sent up a silent prayer that she would not come to retract those words.

"I don't think you did. Hell," he said fiercely, "I know you didn't. You loved me, but you'd never said the words because I'd made it clear I didn't want to hear them." He hesitated. He had to tell her the rest, all of it, but in a way that made her understand he'd loved her, even then. "I don't know exactly why you left me—you didn't leave a note, you didn't leave any kind of message—but I can make a good guess, *habiba*. See, I was away on business. I should have taken you with me, but I didn't. I didn't call you, either, while I was gone, not the way you'd surely have expected, not the way my heart told me to. And when I finally did, you said how you'd missed me. And you told me about a wonderful gift you'd arranged for me—for us." His voice broke. "And I—God, and I cast it aside, I was cruel and cold and—"

Something—thunder?—drowned out his words. They both looked up; a helicopter roared low over their heads, the sound of its rotors filling the sky with noise, its bulk casting a shadow over them and the hot white sand. They watched as it headed over the palms beyond the beach and descended. It dropped from view; the sound of its engines faded, then died, and silence cloaked the island again.

No, he thought desperately, *no, not yet. It was too soon...*

"They've found us," Grace said in a low voice.

Their eyes met, filled not with joy but with trepidation.

Salim nodded. He rose and drew Grace to her feet with him. She was still staring at him; he could see the beat of her pulse in her throat. She shuddered despite the tropical heat, and he picked up one of the big beach towels, shook it free of sand and wrapped it around her shoulders, then wrapped another around his waist.

"There's more to tell," he said quietly.

"That you finally came after me. To Bali. And that's why we were on the plane. You were taking me home with you."

Her words were rushed and desperate with hope, and everything in him wanted to say yes, that was what had happened—but this was no time for lies.

"I went to Bali to find you, *habiba*. And to take you back to New York. But do you remember what I said?" He drew her to him. "That part of what I would tell you was good—and part was bad?"

Grace licked her lips. "And—and the bad part is coming next?"

He nodded. "It is, Grace. *Habiba,* I beg you to listen with an open mind and remember what we've shared these last few days."

She reached out to touch him, hesitated and drew back her hand.

"I will," she said, but doubt was in her voice.

It killed him to hear it. He cursed his cowardice, his selfishness. He should have told her everything last night, while she still lay in his arms, while their bodies were still joined as their heartbeats slowed in the aftermath of their passion…

"Sheikh Salim! Hey, your highness!"

He swung around. Jack and another man, an all-too-familiar man, were running toward them. Automatically he put his arm around Grace, drew her close against him in a protective gesture.

"Sir." Jack beamed from ear to ear as he and the second man reached them. "I got the Sat Com—the satellite communications—up and running right before dawn. Didn't want to get your hopes up but, you can see, it worked. I contacted Sir Edward. And your people. Senahdar, you said, so I got in touch with the palace there."

Salim nodded at the man beside Jack and held out his hand. "Kareem," he said to his father's prime minister.

The minister ignored the proffered hand and dropped to his knees. "My lord. We thought you had been lost in the sea!"

Salim touched the man's shoulder. "Please," he said gently, "stand up, Kareem. There is no need to bow to me. And as you can see, I am fine."

Kareem rose, smiled at his prince—and looked at Grace. His expression went from delight to fury. She stared at him in bewilderment. What had she done to incur such anger?

"And this," the prime minister said coldly, "is the woman. It would have been kismet if she had drowned."

"Kareem! We will talk of this later."

"A thief," the prime minister growled. "An

embezzler. A woman who stole from you and our people…"

"Kareem," Salim roared. "Return to the house. Miss Hudson and I—"

Grace gave a sharp cry as she wrenched free of Salim's encircling arm.

"I remember," she said. "I remember everything. How you made it clear you were tired of me. How I left you, and never mind that nonsense about me not leaving a note. I left a note. I e-mailed it to you. I told you why I was leaving, where I was going—"

"Grace. My beloved—"

He reached for her. She slapped away his hand. Jack cleared his throat; the prime minister snarled with rage and Salim swung toward him, his face dark with fury.

"If you are not gone from here the next time I turn around," he said, in a voice Grace had never heard before, "I will feed your worthless carcass to the sharks!"

The man slunk away. Jack followed after him. Salim took a breath and turned toward Grace.

"*Habiba.* I beg you. Let me explain—"

"There's nothing to explain, your highness."

Her voice trembled, her color was high but she stood straight and tall and proud. "Or maybe I should say, there's no way to talk your way out of this." She stepped closer, her eyes cold and fixed on his. "I'd become a game you'd tired of. I left, hoping—praying—you'd come after me, but you didn't."

"Grace. *Habiba.* These last days—"

"Do not *'habiba'* me, you worthless, selfish, arrogant son of a bitch!" She moved closer still, chin lifted, voice low and humming with anger. "These last days have been the dream of a man like you. A willing woman. No-holds-barred sex, 24/7. Sex, sex and more sex." Tears rose in her eyes; he reached for her and she put her hands against his chest and pushed him hard enough so he stumbled back. "I remember everything, Salim—including why we were on your plane. You were taking me to New York so you could send me to prison."

"Grace. Grace, listen to me—"

"You said I was a thief. That I'd stolen your money. That I was an embezzler."

She was panting with anger, with hatred for this man who had broken her heart not once or twice but three times. How could she have imagined she loved him? How, sweet heaven, how?

"*Habiba*. What can I do to make all this go away?"

So typical. He ruled the world. A wave of his hand, a word, and he could make anything he wanted happen.

But not this time, she thought, even as she feared she might die of the ache in her heart. Not this time, and never again.

"If you have any decency in you," Grace said tonelessly, "you'll get me back to New York and never, ever let me see your face again."

"Grace," he said, and reached toward her.

She jerked back. "I don't want your hands on me," she said. "Do you understand? Your touch makes me feel dirty."

She spun on her heel, strode away from him, and all he could do was watch her. That proud walk. That straight spine. She hated him. Despised him. She was lost to him, forever.

And he had only himself to blame.

He waited a long, long time. Waited until the sun was once again dropping into the sea. Then he went to the house where he had been so happy, told the chopper pilot to ready the aircraft for takeoff, asked Jack to escort Ms. Hudson to the landing pad…

Hours later, they were in Tokyo.

He arranged for Grace to fly to San Francisco. He owed her that.

As for himself—what he owed himself was what he would now have.

A lifetime of emptiness and despair.

CHAPTER TWELVE

June in New York City.

SALIM had always thought it the city's most perfect month. Warm days. Cool nights. Trees in Central Park stretching leafy arms to a sky washed clean by spring rain.

But as the soft days of early summer stole over Manhattan, he hardly noticed. He was busy, far too busy for such nonsense. He was negotiating to purchase a private bank in Abu Dhabi, expanding operations in France.

Who could pay attention to something as frivolous as the change of seasons? Not he. And not his sometime-terrace resident, the red-tailed hawk.

The hawk had been gone by the time he'd returned from Bali and the island—the onset of winter had finally driven the creature away. But he was back now, sitting on the parapet in his usual majestic solitude. If spring was supposed to inspire him to find a mate, it hadn't done so.

The hawk was as impervious to domesticity as Salim.

Who had time or need for spring or females or anything other than one's own responsibilities?

As Salim watched, the red-tail flapped its wings and soared into the sky. Salim turned away to finish dressing for a dinner meeting. It was difficult to find time during the day to discharge his corporate duties, including the hiring of a new CFO to replace Shipley, now facing years in prison.

It had been simple enough to prove his guilt, once everyone stopped looking in the wrong direction. Shipley had the heart and instincts of a thief; when he'd noticed the relationship developing between Salim and Grace, he'd seized what he saw as a golden opportunity and begun plotting a way to use that knowledge to pull off what he'd considered the perfect theft.

He'd been patient, biding his time before hinting to Grace that she was about to be replaced. Luckily for him, she'd already started sensing a change in Salim.

Shipley's sly suggestions that she was on her way out made terrible sense.

The final piece of his plan involved a skill that had nothing to do with finance. It turned out Shipley was a near-genius with computers. He'd been hacking into the company's e-mail for a while, strictly for kicks.

The night Grace fled New York, she sent two e-mails: one to Shipley telling him she was quitting immediately, another to Salim telling him she was leaving him because she knew he didn't want her in his life anymore.

"I have sent the sheikh an e-mail, informing him of my decision," she wrote in her e-mail to Shipley. When he read it, read those words, he saw his chance.

He hacked into the system to delete the e-mail Grace had sent him, found the one she'd sent Salim and deleted it, too. Then he embezzled the ten million dollars via computer, sat back… and waited.

But his scheme had been like a ball of yarn. Once Salim's investigators found a dangling end and tugged, it all came apart.

As for Grace…Salim gave a mental shrug as he knotted his tie.

He would never really forgive himself for believing her guilty. He'd done what he could to make up for it: a couple of discreet phone calls to old university friends on the coast and James Lipton—James Lipton the Fourth, Salim thought with a cold smile—had suddenly found himself not just unemployed but without any significant future career prospects.

Another call to a pal who owned an investment company in San Francisco had secured Grace a vice presidency, though she would never know he'd had a hand in it.

The rest? Those days on the island, the passion, the pleasure…

Salim smoothed down his tie and reached for his dark blue suit jacket.

Sex. Amazing, incredible sex, heightened by their close brush with death and the lush beauty of a tropical paradise. What man and woman could resist such enticement?

But love? He frowned as he took a quick look at himself in the foyer mirror.

No. It had not been love. Actually he'd been

right all along. Their affair had run its course. Perhaps he should have ended things more cleanly all those months ago. Always before, he'd ended affairs with some modicum of polish. A gradual tapering off of contact and then something from Cartier or Tiffany, but his instincts had been on target. Grace was bright, she was beautiful—but the time had come to end things.

He was willing to admit he had not done it properly but nothing more than—

A flash of movement caught his eye. The redtail was swooping toward the parapet but he wasn't alone. A darker, larger bird flew beside him. A female? Salim watched as the two landed on the parapet; his fiercely independent hawk turned to the other, dropped a small kill at her feet, cocked his head and looked at her with what could only be described as hope.

Salim stared at the pair. Then he shook his head and scooped up his car keys. "Good luck, pal," he muttered, and walked briskly to his private elevator.

His cell phone rang as he stepped inside. He checked the number on the screen and smiled. The call was from his old friend, Khalil.

"Hello, stranger," Salim said. "I thought you'd forgotten my number."

"The same to you, old friend. I haven't heard from you since we spoke after you came back from the dead. How are you doing?"

"Fine, just fine. But busy, you know?"

"So I hear. Work, work, work. That's what Tariq and I were just discussing, how you've suddenly turned into an all too serious workaholic. No time to meet up in London last month or to fly down to Aruba two weeks ago, despite our gold-plated invitations."

Salim chuckled. The invitations, in both instances, had been e-mails that had basically said, *Here's where we are, we know you're not a corpse at the bottom of the Pacific anymore so where in hell are you?*

"London's wet in the spring," he said as he stepped from the elevator and nodded to the concierge. "As for islands…I've had my fill of dots of land surrounded by water for a while."

"You don't mean that."

"Every word." Salim mouthed "thanks" to the doorman and walked briskly to the Porsche Carrera GT the parking attendant had left at the curb. "I'm going to stick with my lap pool for the next few months."

"Ah. Too bad. Tariq and I have been looking at property in the Caribbean. Thought we might buy an island, the three of us."

"We just bought land in Colorado."

"Right. For skiing. This would be—"

"You might as well try to sell snow to a polar bear," Salim said as he got behind the wheel of the Porsche and pulled into traffic. "Didn't you hear me the first time? No islands for me."

"Picture it, okay? Low green hills. White sandy beaches. Blue water, green palms—"

An image flashed before Salim. A woman, laughing up at him. A willowy, tawny-maned blonde as lissome as her name.

"No," he said sharply. "Thanks, but I'm not interested."

There was a beat of silence. "You've seen one island, you've seen them all, huh?"

"Something like that."

"Or was it the thought of wives and kids? Too much domesticity, even on an island the size of the one we're looking at?"

"No," Salim said again, "nothing like that. A man wants those things—"

"A wife. Children."

"A man wants them, he's entitled to them. Me, I'm staying with the life I've been living. The one you two baboons forgot. You know. Freedom. Independence."

"And an assortment of babes."

"Exactly." A lie. He hadn't looked at a woman in months. Too busy, was the reason. Far too busy. "Look, I'd love to talk longer but I have an appointment."

"Aha. A hot date. With the lady who was shipwrecked with you?"

"No."

"You're not together?"

"We are not. Why should we be?"

"Well, weren't you and she an item last year? Tariq and I just figured, considering you ended up marooned together—"

"You figured wrong," Salim said flatly.

"Yeah, okay, don't snap my head off. It just seemed logical that—"

"Khalil. I have to go. I told you, I have an app— I have a date."

"How about meeting us for drinks instead?"

"Meeting you for… Where are you?"

"In New York," another voice said.

"Tariq?"

"The one and only."

Salim braked at a red light and checked the street sign. He was a block from the restaurant where his meeting was to take place. "Why didn't you let me know you two were flying in? I'd have kept the evening free."

"Well, neither of us knew until the last minute. How's twenty minutes sound?"

"For what?"

"For getting out of your date and getting your princely self down to that little place in Chelsea. You know the one."

"I can't just cancel at the last second."

"Well, no. You can't. Not so you can see your two oldest friends when you haven't seen them in, what, six, seven months? That's perfectly understandable. How could a date with a woman be more important than the two of us?" Tariq's tone became even more teasing. "Unless, of course, the lady is someone special."

His accountant was hardly special. Even if she had been, meeting with his best friends would have taken precedence.

"Twenty minutes," Salim said, and he disconnected.

It took no time to contact his accountant, offer his apologies and tell her he'd have his P.A. phone to make another appointment. Even if he'd had a date, it wouldn't have taken much longer. You phoned the florist, sent the woman in question three or four dozen long-stemmed roses. The lady would be mollified.

They always were.

He'd never yet dated a woman who couldn't be won over by an apology as long as it was accompanied by a lavish gift.

Except, of course, for Grace.

Okay. All right. He hadn't just put her on that plane in Tokyo, sent her home and forgotten all about her. Idiot that he'd been, still caught up in the whole island thing, he'd sent her flowers. Dozens and dozens of them. And chocolates. Handmade, elegantly wrapped, seemingly endless boxes of chocolates.

And gotten back notes from the children's

wards at two different San Francisco hospitals thanking him for the wonderful gifts.

We have enough flowers to brighten all the children's rooms, the notes said, *and our staff adores the chocolates.*

A diamond bracelet got him an even more effusive note from a home for the aged.

What an amazing gift, it gushed. *We offered it at auction. The profits will completely refurbish our recreation wing.*

That was when he'd faced reality.

Why send a woman a gift if she was going to give it away? Why give her anything when she had no place in your life? Most of all, why not face facts?

The island idyll had been nothing but fiction.

End of story, end of nonsense.

Time to get on with life.

His friends were waiting for him in the rear of the small, dark tavern.

It was not the kind of place anyone would expect to find three billionaire sheikhs, which had always been what they liked about it.

Tariq and Khalil rose as he approached the

table they'd commandeered. Handshakes. Slaps on the back. Then, finally, the kinds of hugs men give each other when their lives have been entwined for so long they are more brothers than friends.

"We ordered for you," Tariq said. "A porterhouse, rare. Baked potato. Green salad. Dos Equis."

"Great. Excellent. By Ishtar, it's good to see the two of you. You're right, it's been months."

"Busy months," Khalil said.

"Productive ones," Tariq added.

The men grinned at each other. Salim sat back as the waiter put a chilled bottle of beer in front of him. He waved away the offered mug and looked from one smiling face to the other. His pals looked like a pair of Cheshire cats.

He told them so.

Tariq laughed. "Wrong species. Try a pair of stallions."

"Studly and gorgeous as always," Khalil said smugly. "We're both having babies. Tariq's second, my first. Well, Madison and Layla are having babies. Hell. You know what I mean."

Salim smiled and held out his beer bottle. "Congratulations," he said, as the men touched the bottles together. "You two don't believe in wasting time."

"Life is short," Tariq said, his smile tilting. "Wasting time is the ultimate mistake."

Salim and Khalil nodded. They knew he was thinking of his brother, who had died in an accident a couple of years before. They sat in silence for a few seconds. Then, Khalil cleared his throat.

"So. That was one hell of a thing, what happened to you."

"You were damned lucky."

"Yeah." Salim took a long breath. "My crew wasn't."

"It was a miracle anyone got out alive. You and the woman—did we ever meet her?"

"No."

"But she was your mistress for several months."

"She was my lover," Salim countered sharply. "Not my mistress."

Khalil and Tariq looked at each other, eyebrows raised.

"Uh, sure. Your lover. That's what I meant. What was her name?"

"Grace," Salim said, and tilted his beer bottle to his lips. "Grace Hudson."

"Right. When we talked to you after your rescue, you never mentioned that you'd saved her life. But when we read about your CFO pleading guilty to embezzlement, that he'd framed the Hudson woman for it—"

"What do the papers ever know?"

"Well, of course, but the *Times* said—"

"Can we talk about something else?"

Another quick exchange of looks. Something was going on here. Tariq and Khalil had already agreed on that. Both had talked with Salim immediately after he'd been rescued; both had gotten the same runaround. He had survived the crash, he felt fine, he'd ordered a new plane and quietly done everything possible for the loved ones his crew had left behind and, when they'd asked about Grace Hudson, those very same words.

Could they please talk about something else?

They could, but they didn't want to.

Their questions about Grace had not been as casually presented as they'd sounded. Whatever was wrong had something to do with her and at the urging of their wives—the women had become close friends—they were on what Layla and Madison called a sort of intervention.

The men would never use such a psychobabble term but, damn it, they knew that's what it was.

Salim had buried himself in work. He'd always worked hard—they all did—but he'd also played hard. Not anymore. They didn't for a moment believe he'd had a date tonight. Like a monk, he seemed to have given up women.

Tariq raised his eyebrows at Khalil. Khalil scowled and jerked his head toward Salim. *You do it,* the gesture said. *No, you do it,* the answering emphatic frown replied. Salim, meanwhile, looked from one of them to the other.

"Have you become bobble-head dolls, or are you going to tell me what's going on here?"

"Nothing's going on here," Tariq replied innocently.

"Nothing at all," Khalil added.

Silence. Then both men spoke at once. "Damn it, man," Tariq growled just as Khalil grumbled, "What the hell, Salim!" And Salim, who knew them as well as he knew himself, sat back, put down his beer, folded his arms and glowered.

"All right, let's have it. What are you doing in New York?"

"We're here on, uh, on business."

"Monkey business." Salim's mouth thinned. "We've been friends too long to play games. Why are you here?"

And they told him. In short, succinct sentences. They said he had not been the same since the accident. No, that wasn't correct. Actually he hadn't been the same since a business trip to the coast last year, or maybe since he'd broken up with Grace Hudson right about that same time, and when he'd been seeing her, hadn't he called her his mistress when they'd called her his lover and now, not ten minutes ago, hadn't it been *he* who'd corrected *them?*

So, who was this woman? What was she? And what had she done to mess with his head?

"All right," Salim said tightly, "Okay! You can stop the interrogation. You want the whole ugly story? Here it is."

He began with his initial affair with Grace. About her leaving him and his part in that. About her supposed embezzlement of his ten million. About following her to Bali, almost forcing her onto his plane, the crash, her amnesia, his growing certainty that she had never stolen so much as a dime.

"And then I realized the truth." His voice fell

to a low growl; Tariq and Khalil had to lean in to hear him. "I loved her. I'd always loved her. Hell," he said, his eyes going from one man to the next, his expression daring them to laugh, "I adored her." He paused. "I still do."

No one spoke. Then Tariq cleared his throat. "Well, then, what's the problem? If you love her—"

"She hates me." His voice roughened. "Why wouldn't she? Instead of trusting my instincts, I rushed to judgment."

"Yeah, but she didn't leave you much choice," Khalil said sensibly. "I mean, your reactions were logical, Salim. She ran away, the money was missing…"

"Didn't you hear what I said? I love her. I loved her all the time. If I'd admitted it to myself, if I hadn't been such an arrogant—"

Khalil opened his mouth to answer. Tariq shook his head. You didn't use reason when you were dealing with a man in love; who knew that better than they?

"You've tried talking to her?" Tariq said softly.

Salim gave a bitter laugh. "I must have left a dozen messages on her voice mail."

"Flowers? Candy? Jewelry?"

"Yes, yes and yes. She gave everything to charity. I should have figured she would. She never wanted the things I bought her in the past." He wrapped his hands around his bottle of beer. "She isn't much for material things, you know?"

They knew. Their wives weren't, either.

"But she loved what I gave her when we were on the island. Well, what she said I gave her. A sky alive with shooting stars…" Salim's words trailed away. His face lit with hope. "Stars," he said, "damn it, stars!"

He shot to his feet. Went around the table just as Khalil and Tariq rose from their chairs.

"Thank you," he said happily.

They looked at each other, then at him.

"For what?" Tariq asked.

Salim grinned from ear to ear. Grabbed each man's face and planted a smacking kiss on each forehead.

"Hey!" they said, jerking back.

Salim ran for the door.

Why would anyone want to live in San Francisco?

There'd been a time Grace had wanted just

that, but it had been a passing thought during a long-ago holiday. Now that the city was her home, she couldn't think of one good reason to be happy about it.

It was mid-June and here she was, huddling in a raincoat as she trudged up a steep hill after foolishly telling her driver it was late and she wouldn't need him any more that evening. The wind blowing off the bay was wet and cold and so was she—but then, she never felt warm lately. How could she, when the weather was so damned miserable and she was working so hard she had no time to think?

A lie.

She had lots of time to think. Endless nights of thinking, lying awake, thinking about what had happened to her. What two men had done to her: one who'd set her up to seem like a thief and one who'd hurt her so deeply she had no difficulty believing there really were such things as broken hearts.

Shipley, at least, was paying for what he'd done. He was in prison, and would be for a very long time.

Salim was paying no price at all. A man like

him never would. He'd go through life getting whatever he wanted and those rare times he couldn't, he'd be completely bewildered. Those gifts he'd sent. The messages on her voice mail. Not that she'd played any of them through. She hit Delete at the sound of his voice.

He was, as the saying went, history. It was time to move on.

Her apartment was on the second floor in a Victorian mansion just off Telegraph Hill. She dug her key from her purse, unlocked the front door, climbed the steps to her flat—

And stood still.

There was a box on the doormat in front of her door.

No. Not again. Salim had given up trying to bribe her back into his bed; there hadn't been flowers or chocolates or a bracelet so beautiful it had stolen her breath away in weeks and weeks and…

It didn't have to be from him. In fact, it couldn't be from him. Everything he'd sent had come by courier, the boxes magnificently wrapped and tied with gold and silver bows. This package must have been left here by mistake. Or it could be something she'd ordered but no, it couldn't because she hadn't ordered anything and even if she had, the delivery guy or the postman would have left it on the porch…

Grace rolled her eyes, snatched up the box, stabbed her key in the lock and flung open her door.

"For heaven's sake," she said aloud, "just open the damned thing, see what it is and if it's from him, figure out what charity could use it."

She shrugged off her coat. Dumped it on a chair. Sat on the sofa, undid the plain brown twine on the parcel, then the equally plain brown paper to reveal a square white box. No gold leaf. No satin ribbon. Just a box.

"It's just a box, *habiba*."

Her head shot up. Salim stood in the open doorway, big and beautiful and not a dream because when she dreamed of him, he never looked like this, as if the world hung waiting on what might happen next. And yet, in those dreams, her heart raced as it did now, her eyes drank him in…

Stop it!

He didn't mean a thing to her. She had to remember that, she told herself as she rose to her feet, the box in her hands.

"What are you doing here?"

"I came to see you," he said calmly. "To talk to you."

"Well, you've seen me. And talked to me." She held out the box. "So take your—your whatever it is and go away."

He didn't go away. Instead he shut the door and moved slowly toward her. She wanted to turn and run. He wouldn't harm her physically; she knew that. But if he touched her—if he touched her, she might slug him. Heaven knew, she'd thought about it often enough, wished she'd done it that day, that awful day she'd finally remembered what he had done to her, how he had drawn away from her before that trip to the coast, how he had rejected her simple offering of a weekend alone together...

How he'd so readily believed she was a thief.

"Grace," he said softly.

She bit back a moan because now, with him so near her, his pale eyes locked to her face, she knew that she didn't want to send him away. She wanted to throw herself into his arms, ask him if it was true, what he'd said on the island, that he loved her, he would always love her...

"Grace. I know I don't deserve a second chance but... Will you do one thing for me, *habiba?* Will you open that box?"

"What for?" she said, damning herself for the tremor in her voice. "I don't want whatever's in it, Salim, no matter what it cost."

Salim yearned to touch her but he knew it would be a mistake. She had to want him. If she didn't—if she didn't, he was lost.

"Open it, *habiba*. And if you truly do not want what it contains, I will go away and live the rest of my life with an empty heart." His voice dropped. "With a broken heart, sweetheart, but if that is your choice, I will respect it."

"Talk," she said, looking away from him because watching him hurt her heart. Her hands shook as she lifted the lid of the box and unfolded the white tissue paper inside. "Nothing but talk. And you're good at talk. Good at telling lies. At saying things you think I want to hear, things that will—that will—"

Grace stared at the object inside the box. It was a glass globe. A snow globe. A child's toy.

No, she thought, lifting it in her cupped hands. Not a toy. This was far too beautiful for that.

The globe held a perfect miniature of the island where they'd spent three perfect days. A house, a tiny replica of the one overlooking the sea. A gentle slope leading down to palm trees bordering a stretch of glittering white sand and beyond it, the gleam of blue ocean.

One curving wall of the globe was silken black, hung with a round ivory moon.

She looked up, bewildered. "It's the island."

"We were happy there, *habiba,*" Salim said softly. He had closed the remaining space that separated them; if she raised her hand, she could touch him. "Happy—and deeply in love."

"In lust," Grace said, trying to sound as if she didn't care when oh God, she did, she did…

Her hands were curved around the globe. Salim lightly covered them with his.

"Shake the globe." he whispered. Her eyes met his and he smiled. "Shake it, *habiba.* Please."

His hands fell away. Slowly she lifted the globe and shook it, and her soft cry of delighted surprise went straight to his heart.

What looked like millions of tiny diamonds seemed to swirl from the black silk sky and into the perfect blue sea.

"Oh," Grace looked up, her eyes filled with delight. "Oh, Salim…"

"A sky alive with shooting stars, beloved. Do you remember that night, how we made love?" He took her face in his hands. "I'll never look at the night sky again, *habiba,* without remembering how much I love you."

"Salim." Tears streamed down her face. "Salim, how could you have thought I'd steal from you?"

"A man determined to be blind to love is capable of great stupidity, sweetheart."

"I loved you. With all my heart. I always knew you didn't love me and I thought I could live with that but then you changed, you began treating me as if you were tired of me. And then you went to California…"

Salim took the globe from her hands and set it aside.

"I love you," he said roughly. "I adore you. Please, Grace, give me your heart as I give you mine."

She looked deep into his eyes. He held his breath; he thought the world might be holding its breath, too. And then she sighed.

"It was my fault, too," she said softly.

"No. I was the one—"

Grace put a finger lightly across his lips. "I shouldn't have run, Salim. I should have waited for you to come home and then confronted you, asked you if you were tired of our relationship. Instead, I behaved like a child and ran away. It's just that I loved you so much, so very much…"

"Can you love me again, *habiba?*"

Her lips curved in a smile. "I never stopped loving you," she whispered.

Salim bent his head and kissed her. She looped her arms around his neck and kissed him back. When the kiss finally ended, he framed her face with his hands.

"I want to live all the days and nights of my life with you," he said softly.

Grace laughed. "Is that a proposal, your highness?"

"It is a command," Salim said in his most imperious voice. "You will marry me and be my love forever, or—"

"Or?"

"Or my heart will surely break."

"Never," she whispered. "We will never

break each other's hearts again, my love. Never, never—"

"Never," Salim said, and he lifted Grace in his arms, carried her to the bedroom, and they sealed their vows in the wonder of being joined not just by passion but by love.

EPILOGUE

THEY were married two weeks later, on the beautiful beach on Dilarang Island. The wedding took place at dusk. Torches flamed brightly against the darkening sky.

Sir Edward Brompton said he was delighted to see his island play the part of Cupid; he and his wife and toddler daughter were honored guests. Tariq and Khalil were Salim's best men; Layla and Madison were thrilled to be Grace's matrons of honor. They said they felt as if they'd known her all their lives and Grace laughed through happy tears and told them she felt the same way.

Grace wore a long white gown of lace and silk, custom-made in Paris. Her tawny hair hung loose on her bare shoulders. She carried a bouquet of tiny pink and white orchids from the mansion's garden. Salim wore a black dinner jacket, a ruffled white shirt and dark trousers.

Both of them were barefoot.

Salim had told his bride she could have any kind of wedding she wanted and this simple, lovely ceremony that included vows they had written themselves had been her choice.

When the ceremony ended, Tariq's little boy plopped down in the sand with the Brompton's little girl and made sand castles under the smiling, watchful eyes of their parents. The small group of invited guests, including Salim's father and the prime minister, dined on champagne and lobster. A quartet of tuxedoed but barefoot musicians played until midnight, when the happily exhausted guests all trooped to their rooms in the mansion.

The babies, of course, had given out long before that.

Grace and Salim stayed in the suite where they'd finally admitted their love for each other. But in the deepest, darkest part of the night they slipped away, got into a pink and white Jeep and drove to the waterfall where they'd almost made love so many months ago.

Grace wore a sarong; she'd put flowers from

her bridal bouquet in her hair. Salim wore low-slung jeans. As for the waterfall…it wore a necklace of moonlight.

They made love. Tenderly. Passionately. After, as Grace lay safe in Salim's arms, a brilliant light shot across the black silk sky.

"Look," Grace said with delight. "A shooting star!" She rolled on top of her husband, linked her hands behind his neck and batted her lashes. "Did you arrange for that to happen, my sheikh?"

He grinned. "There are some things even I can't take credit for, *habiba*." His smile faded; he gave her a slow, deep kiss. "Like finding you."

Grace cupped Salim's face. "I love you," she whispered. "I'll always love you, Salim, always—"

He kissed her and more stars flamed across the night sky.

Who could blame the lovers for thinking the universe was smiling in agreement?

0509 Rom LP

MILLS & BOON PUBLISH EIGHT LARGE PRINT TITLES A MONTH. THESE ARE THE EIGHT TITLES FOR JUNE 2009.

❧

THE RUTHLESS MAGNATE'S VIRGIN MISTRESS
Lynne Graham

THE GREEK'S FORCED BRIDE
Michelle Reid

THE SHEIKH'S REBELLIOUS MISTRESS
Sandra Marton

THE PRINCE'S WAITRESS WIFE
Sarah Morgan

THE AUSTRALIAN'S SOCIETY BRIDE
Margaret Way

THE ROYAL MARRIAGE ARRANGEMENT
Rebecca Winters

TWO LITTLE MIRACLES
Caroline Anderson

MANHATTAN BOSS, DIAMOND PROPOSAL
Trish Wylie

MILLS & BOON®
Pure reading pleasure™

MILLS & BOON PUBLISH EIGHT LARGE PRINT TITLES A MONTH. THESE ARE THE EIGHT TITLES FOR JULY 2009.

MILLS & BOON

Pure reading pleasure™